ROSE LEGACY

An Evans Novel of Romance

ROSE LEGACY

DIANE CAREY

M Evans
Lanham • New York • Boulder • Toronto • Plymouth, UK

M. Evans
An imprint of The Rowman & Littlefield Publishing Group, Inc.
4501 Forbes Boulevard, Suite 200, Lanham, Maryland 20706
http://www.rlpgtrade.com

10 Thornbury Road, Plymouth PL6 7PP, United Kingdom

Distributed by National Book Network

First Rowman & Littlefield paperback edition 2014

British Library Cataloguing in Publication Information Available

Library of Congress Cataloging-in-Publication Data Available

ISBN 13: 978-1-59077-372-7 (pbk: alk. paper)

∞™ The paper used in this publication meets the minimum requirements of American National Standard for Information Sciences—Permanence of Paper for Printed Library Materials, ANSI/NISO Z39.48-1992.

Printed in the United States of America

Chapter One

ROSE MACKENZIE PRESSED her hand against the story-tall windows of the Coachman Long Island and stared off at the city. Beyond the putting green the endless lights of Manhattan stretched on in stratified layers. But here, on this private veranda, she was safe and secluded from the other restaurant patrons by a delicate jungle of potted foliage. Outside, the moonlit green tapestry of the golf course looked surreal, as if it were a land of fantasy.

What would it be like? How would it feel to walk into the restaurant like a normal person, to pick her own table, to be served by waiters who didn't know exactly what she liked and disliked? And wouldn't it be fun to refuse the White Russian and order a nice, sloppy Budweiser, then watch the stuffy maitre d's face fall as Red MacKenzie's granddaughter licked the foam from her upper lip?

Instead, Rose sat down and raised the White Russian to her perfectly glossed lips with a quiet sigh. No nerve. No nerve at all. Her jewel-green eyes drifted to the crushed ice drowning in her glass. She needed to socialize more, yes. But maybe Phil was right. Maybe this was a flaky way to go about it.

Soon she'd have no choice but to accept the fact that she'd been stood up. And not for the first time—unfortunately. Plenty of men asked her out only to flag at the last minute. *Am I that bad to look at?* Instantly she knew what Phil would say: "*No, Rose, you're that* good *to look at. Tall, gorgeous women are intimidating.*

Even as she heard her imagination play that recording, she knew she wasn't all that gorgeous; in fact, her face was rather plain and underplayed. She liked it that way. Despite the temptation to overuse make-up, she had always settled for mascara to darken the light cayenne-colored lashes, and lip gloss to bring her mouth out of hiding on her ruddy Scots complexion. Her height—yes, that had always intimidated people. Her sleek, blunt-cut red hair would almost brush a six-foot door frame, and her long-boned body simply added to the illusion of great height. Phil always told her there was something innately sensual about a woman who was taller than other women, and Rose had always carried her height like a crown, wearing heels, and donning only bold colors. Because Red MacKenzie had been over six foot three himself, his lanky granddaughter hadn't been too self-conscious about her height, at least not until Red died and she suddenly found herself in charge of the Coachman chain some seven years ago.

"Ms. MacKenzie?"

She blinked. Aaron, the maitre d', stood beside the table, hesitantly leaning toward her. "Yes, Aaron?"

"A message for you, ma'am." He presented a little silver tray with a little white envelope.

"Of course," she said, pursing her lips as she unsheathed the telegram. From her date. Sorry, had to leave country on business. Stop. Perhaps next month. Stop. Bye. Stop.

"Stop is right," Rose murmured. "I must really be doing something wrong."

"Pardon, ma'am?" Aaron leaned closer, carefully pretending he didn't know what was in the message.

"Nothing." She crumpled the telegram and dropped it back onto the pretentious little tray. "Aaron, would you please find Mr. Van Dyke and have him join me here?"

He nodded. "Right away, Ms. MacKenzie."

"Fast enough for you?"

Turning toward the familiar voice, she found herself smiling up at Phil.

The diffused dining room light brushed across the lines of what he called his "negotiation suit," the double-breasted jacket giving authority to his slimness. The camel brown color and windowpane pattern added a richness that echoed from his brown hair right down to his cap-toed shoes.

"That's what I call quick work. Guess I didn't realize the extent of my power," she teased.

"You never have, Rose," Phil said as he took the seat next to her and nodded to Aaron. "My usual, Aaron."

"Immediately, sir."

"I know I'm not supposed to be here," Phil said, "and I'll scoot before your date arrives, I promise. But there are two items we should discuss. First, I wanted to remind you about the auction Friday at the museum. You promised Willoughby Henderson you would attend. You haven't forgotten, have you?"

Rose cleared her throat. "The auction?" she responded. "Of course not. How could I forget something like that? I'll be there with bells on."

"Second," Phil continued, "I need the sketches for the new Coachman, and I'll bet my best tie that you've got them right down there in your case."

"Oh, you bet right." Rose reached down for her briefcase, snapped it open, and extracted a thin leather folder. "And they're stunning! I can't wait till we start building. It's going to resemble a castle."

"You sound like a little girl who just met Santa," Phil murmured. He cleared his throat. "If only the preliminaries weren't such a pain." He took the folder and thumbed through its contents.

"You love them," she accused, "every bit as much as I do."

"Guilty. But, listen. I just finished talking to the contractor. Fusero says he's in a financial bind of some sort. Did you hear anything about this? He's come in with the lowest bid, but he says he's losing money on it."

Rose clunked her drink down on the linen tablecloth. "Phil, you didn't fall for that, did you?"

His brown eyes blinked. He paused, suddenly looking innocent. "Uh...did I?"

"Phil, you'll never learn to quit being such a sweetheart." She flagged down a passing waiter and requested a phone.

"Losing money, my eye. Fusero just bought all new equipment and now he wants me to think he's doing us a favor so I'll owe him one. Then he'll be in a position to strong-arm me on the next job."

Aaron appeared bearing a white streamline telephone and a snifter of brandy for Phil. Without a word Rose scooped up the phone and pecked out a number.

"Losing money," she muttered, grinning at Phil as he watched her in knowing silence. She crossed her legs, patiently waiting for Fusero to pick up the line.

Phil settled back with his brandy and an expression of awe, prepared to watch a master of negotiation in action.

"Gene?" Rose's face lit up as the tourney began. "How are you? Yes, Phil just told me your bid's the best on the Coachman Dallas. Yes, it's very reasonable. But he tells me you're losing money on the job. Is that right?... I see. I understand... well, that makes sense, certainly, but it puts me in a peculiar position. Gene, if you're *losing* money, I just can't do business with you. I have a policy never to do business with contractors who are working at a loss."

As Rose paused, Phil figured there was some serious whining and wailing going on somewhere near Dallas.

"Yes," Rose murmured patiently. "I'm really sorry about this, but I don't want the responsibility. We've been burned before when people who were losing money did a slipshod job and... Oh, no, I know *you* wouldn't do that, but what can I tell my stockholders?... And I certainly wouldn't want to put you in that position either." She pursed her lips, trying to keep from giggling as she watched Phil beam with amusement.

"Gene, you don't want me to break my own rule, do you? Look, I want you to do the job. I like your work, okay? I really do. Couldn't you just... lie, or something? Couldn't we pretend you're not losing money? Well, what do you mean? Are you losing money or not? Yes, I'll wait." She cupped her hand over the mouthpiece and lounged back. "He's got me on hold—he's rechecking his figures."

Phil pressed his knuckles to his mouth to hold the laughter in. Rose was an amazing performer, not only good at what she did, but in love with it as well. Red MacKenzie might have started the chain of luxury restaurant/golf resorts, but it was his whip-sharp granddaughter who had tripled the stock value in only seven years. Tonight's negotiation was a golden example of how she'd done it.

"Yes, Gene, I'm still here," Rose answered. "Oh? Oh, that's wonderful. I'm so glad. Oh, of course... everybody miscalculates from time to time. You're not just telling me this, are you? I'm really sticking my neck out after what you told Phil.... All right, Gene. And Gene, if you're lying, I'll keep the secret. I really *want* you.... Yes. But you *owe* me one. Okay. Yes, I will...you, too."

"I'll bet he's calling you everything but a nice lady right now," Phil offered.

"Choice adjectives and creative nouns, I betcha," she agreed, swirling the ice around in her glass. "But we won."

"Rose, you just blind me sometimes. I don't know how you can be so coldblooded and still be so—"

"Now, Phil—"

"Cute. I was going to say cute."

"Sure you were."

Phil tucked the folder under his arm and scooped up his brandy. "I'll get out of here. I shouldn't be here when your date shows up—"

Rose suddenly grabbed his hand. "No, Phil, wait. Please don't go."

The mood changed, abruptly and completely. He paused, reading something in her eyes that had overtones of despair. "Why not?" he asked.

Rose withdrew her fingers from his wrist. "He's not coming." She rested one long forearm on the table before her. "Ducked out on me."

Settling slowly back into his chair, Phil murmured, "Oh."

She stared at her drink, noting the way the glass bent her reflection. "Phil, this drink is laughing at me."

He smiled, "Have it flogged. That's what heiresses do best, you know."

"I'm not an heiress anymore," she pointed out. "I'm the queen."

It would have been a pompous statement coming from anyone else, but Rose said it without pride, without joy.

"Well, does that mean we're stuck with each other?" Phil asked.

Rose smiled at his attempt to lighten the gloom, and Phil felt his muscles tighten under the direct assault of her green eyes. If fire was green, it would be the color of Rose MacKenzie's eyes.

"Phil, I'm making a mess of this," she admitted suddenly, giving in to the urge to blurt out her feelings to him. "I don't even know what to do on a date. I should've learned that when I was fifteen, not thirty-one. I don't know what it's like to be with a man on a nonbusiness level. I feel like I'm in a glass booth, *watching* my dates instead of participating in them. How am I ever going to have a family? I have a responsibility to my grandfather's legacy to give him heirs, and I can't even date a man without feeling obligated to entertain him. I learned how to run the business; I should be able to learn how to socialize. What've I done to my life?"

Phil lounged back and tried to look relaxed. "I'll tell you what you've done. You've sacrificed yourself to success. You just said it, right then. You've got a responsibility to Red's legacy." He gripped the edge of the table and leaned forward, his dark eyes intent on her. "But, you don't. You don't. You feel nervous with men because you can't forget who and what you are long enough to think about yourself as a person, not a corporation. Rose, you never expected to inherit the business when you were still so young. After all, Red was sixty-five going on forty. Nobody expected him to die so suddenly. You had to change from a peacock into a shark in about a month and a half, and you're still the shark."

She scooped a lump of ice from her drink and pitched it at him. Her lips curled in a self-conscious grin. "Don't lecture me, you shyster."

He volleyed the ice chip right back at her. "Well? Am I wrong?"

"Was *I* wrong?" she returned immediately. "I did what I had to do."

Phil nodded sympathetically. "I know you did."

He was right; Rose knew that. Her grandfather had been the focus of MacKenzie and Family Enterprises and the Royal Coachman International Incorporated. But suddenly one day he was gone and she had become the new focus—the focus of a multitude of greedy manipulators who saw a young, untried girl running the business. In the midst of her grief she'd suddenly found herself in charge, and in danger. Some of Red MacKenzie's most trusted people had tried to buy her out, pressure her, steer her.

Only Phil's steady presence had kept her from being eaten alive as she struggled to wield the control she had inherited. All too soon the naive girl had been transformed into a stunning businesswoman who trusted few and shunned many. She'd developed a demeanor she only now realized was a form of intimidation. But the armor that protected her business persona also had thwarted her social life.

She longed for a husband and children. She realized she had saved Red's business for his progeny, but she had failed to provide the progeny.

Rose pressed her lips together, scolding herself. Thinking in dollar signs again. She averted her eyes from Phil, knowing he could read the thoughts behind them.

Phil was right—she had reacted to being surrounded by enemies. Everything was a challenge, from the simplest hello to the most complex strategy. She'd known she had to fight, so she'd learned to. Was she still fighting after the ground had been won? Now she didn't know how to make friends anymore. She'd made the decision years ago to abandon her social life, when it became clear that Phil was the only person she could trust. They'd been raised together and thought of each other as siblings.

But he wasn't her brother. Why didn't she just marry him and be done with it?

I couldn't do that to him, she thought, still avoiding looking at him. *Part of me is still waiting for the fire.*

"I owe it to Gran to have a family of my own," she murmured, staring with unfocused eyes at the luxurious tartan carpet. "He raised us, Phil. He gave us everything. And I owe it to myself. I want to be more than just the president of Royal Coachman International and MacKenzie and Family Enterprises. I don't need the kind of life that appears in every issue of *Town & Country*. I just want a family."

Phil nodded. "It takes time, Rose."

"Not this much time. I feel like a clumsy teenager."

"Maybe so, but I'm still going to look after you. I'm going to check out every guy who comes within ten feet of you. Red left you in my trust, and I'm going to make good."

Rose's eyelids tightened, narrowing her emerald eyes with bladelike symmetry. She smiled thoughtfully. "Isn't it pathetic how much we loved that old rattlesnake?"

Phil tipped his head. "I miss him. Always will."

She pressed her hand in his, and he focused on shapely fingernails tinted with russet polish, catching a whiff of the perfume he'd given her for Christmas.

Intrigue, it was called. How carefully he'd chosen it...

"I miss him, too," she said. "He wanted a great-grandchild so badly ...I've thought over the years of having that child, but I never noticed those years slipping away."

Phil swallowed. "Any toad with brains could run Coachman. The only person who can build another MacKenzie for the world is Rose MacKenzie. Only a woman can do that. And you're all woman, Rose."

She raised a hand to his cheek. The candlelight flickered between them.

Phil's parents had managed Red MacKenzie's household and they'd been the closest approximation to parents that Rose had ever known. The Van Dykes had been Red's only "family," except for his strong-willed little granddaughter.

Phil had always tried to protect her, but she'd bested him at every childhood game. By the time puberty rolled around, he'd quit trying to win her heart with his male prowess. Phil just wasn't the knight-in-armor type.

And Rose MacKenzie was a firebrand. She soon outran Phil Van Dyke. He'd watched her go, and she still remembered the looks he'd given her during those tender years.

I probably do love him, she reflected as she looked at him with that brazen honesty that was typical of her. He was the secret crush that had faded but would always remain precious, like a special page in a diary—impossible to relive, but nonetheless cherished.

"Ma'am?"

Rose blinked, then looked up at Aaron. "Yes"

He stepped a little closer. "A gentleman to see you. He asked me to present this."

Aaron's thin hand held a single rose. It was lush and only a bud, and it was blue—deep, shameless azure. No vase, no tissue, no foil. Just a blue rosebud with a long stem—and thorns.

Rose plucked it from the aged hand.

"Nice," she said, disguising her fascination in a flat tone. "But who is it from?"

Aaron's face flushed, and he raised an arrogant eyebrow. "A gentleman outside—he's not a member, ma'am. Shall I have him expelled?"

"Patience, Aaron," Rose admonished. "Bring him over. I want to see what comes with this."

Aaron disappeared again and Rose turned to Phil. "A blue rose?"

Phil shrugged. "No idea, I swear."

"None at all?"

"Nothing!"

Rose felt her spine tingle. She peered through the wall of ferns into the darkened lounge, and wondered.

"Ma'am"—

"Yes, Aaron?"

"The gentleman says he prefers not to come to the table."

"I beg your pardon?"

Aaron's face twitched. "He requests you meet him in the lobby."

Phil stared at the maitre d', then, shifted in his chair. "I'll go Rose."

Her hand shot out toward him. "No."

He hesitated. "What?"

"I'll go."

Phil stood up and hovered over his chair as she got up and smoothed her taffeta skirt. "Do you want— "

"No. I'll go alone."

She stepped past him, hoping he would miss the uncertainty in her eyes. Rose followed Aaron into the lobby, a walnut-paneled parlor with velvet loveseats in emerald green and wallpaper with the sheen of silk. It was empty.

"Aaron?"

The man's eyes widened, then squinted. He peered across the lobby, whirled around to scan the restaurant, ducked out the door to the parking lot, then ducked back in. "Ma'am, I'm afraid he's— "

Rose pressed her lips together. "Couldn't have been very important, could it?"

"But he *was* here!" Aaron angrily insisted.

"I believe you," she said sedately. "It's all right. It's not your fault. Mr. Van Dyke and I will have a light dinner now."

Aaron bowed. "Very good, ma'am. I'm terribly sorry for this."

"Not your fault, Aaron," she tossed back as she turned toward the dining room once again, then stopped short. Behind her, she heard Aaron's subdued gasp.

At the entrance to the main dining room, tucked respectfully against the lush wallpaper, was a bud vase. In it a fan of blue rosebuds made a simple statement against the green tones in the parlor.

Even from where she stood, Rose could see there was no card, no signature, no way to tell the identity of this man who'd fleetingly left a memory on her doorstep.

Yet the message was clear in some hidden part of her mind: *There will soon be something to remember.*

Chapter Two

It might have been the little girl within her—the one who still believed in Rapunzel and rampion and promises, and towers from which golden tresses fell for princes to climb. It might have been the teenager who dreamed of first kisses and long nights dancing endless waltzes in the arms of a man with blue roses.

For whatever inexplicable reason, Rose couldn't forget those Nile-blue roses turning their closed lips up to her, serrated leaves quivering on long thorny stems, glowing in the halo of light cast from the parlor chandelier.

She couldn't forget. Not that night, not the next. Or the next.

Couldn't forget, because the roses wouldn't let her.

On her way up to her penthouse the next night, she was met by a single blue bloom in her private elevator—the one that needed a pass key. Rose had scooped up the bloom and brought it home.

Phil immediately launched an investigation into how this rosebud Zorro had violated building security, but there were no answers. Somehow, a wraith was dropping blue roses in her path.

After meetings the next day at the Coachman Long Island, dinner was quietly served to her and three business associates whose presence was important enough to make her forget the mysterious roses. Rose was doubly jarred when she parted her roll from the warm wrapped basket on the table, and discovered a bottle of perfume actually baked into the bread. *Blue Velvet*, it said. And there was one in each roll.

Everyone at the table now had perfume, and Rose had a blooming mystery.

"I want it stopped, Phil, do you understand? I want it stopped."

"Rose, we could stop it if we knew *how* he's doing these things," Phil admitted as he sat on the edge of her desk in the office above the restaurant. He clasped his hands together, feeling inadequate. "We have a description of him from Aaron, but though he's a great maitre d', he isn't all that observant. He says the man is tall, but from Aaron's point of view, so is Mickey Mouse. We know he's blond. Eyes green or blue, and he was wearing clothes Aaron describes as 'appropriate.' I've notified the police and our private security, but until he commits a crime, we can't take much action."

"Oh, great."

"Whoever he is, you have to admire his ingenuity. He's persistent."

"He's irritating. These situations are getting embarrassing. I can take anything but humiliation, and I don't like being haunted by some conceited would-be boyfriend who likes to play games."

She had finally paced the knotty tension out of her legs, but the haunted feeling remained.

As she spoke, Phil plucked up the latest arrival, a stemless open bloom that had greeted her from a disturbing place this morning—inside her briefcase as she'd opened it to begin her day. As Phil sat there on the wide mahogany desk, he brushed the velvety petals with one finger and murmured, "Where do you supposed he gets blue ones?"

Rose spun around abruptly and leaned across the desk, snatching the large blue flower from Phil's palm.

"Can we please be serious?"

He spread his hands. "I *am* being serious. Where would anybody get roses that color? Maybe if we find out what his source is, we can find his identity."

Rose blinked, then snapped her fingers. "That's brilliant! This blue rose can't be too common. Get on it, would you? Check all the floral sources in the New York area. Somebody must know, right?"

"That's right," Phil said. He slid off the edge of the desk and headed for the door. "I'll let you know what I find out."

"I'll love you forever," she vowed as he swung the door open.

He smiled. "If only it were so."

When Phil left, thoughts of her grandfather filled Rose's mind—a man whom so few men could match in her esteem. He'd left her with a rosey future—and a thorny financial empire.

The comfort was wonderful, but Rose had a recurring nightmare of herself at fifty years old, drinking too much and having affairs with gold-digging tennis instructors, roving endlessly from the Coachman Long Island to the Coachman Paris, to the Coachman Copenhagen, to the one in Dublin, to the one in Dallas, to the one in New Orleans...becoming the loaded spinster of international cuisine.

Do I hate it? she wondered inwardly. No. She couldn't hate anything Gran worked so hard to build. *And he did it for me—his pride and joy.*

She and Red MacKenzie had been a special pair. She'd been as interested in his business dealings as in Barbie dolls and boys. Perhaps some inner wisdom had told her she would someday have to be ready to become president of MacKenzie and Family. Early on she had been ready to prove herself more than merely a beautiful wooden figurehead controlled by surrogates and advisors.

After all, she had been the "Family" part of MacKenzie and Family. *Good old Gran*, she mused as Red MacKenzie's weatherworn face floated across her mind. *He never tried to protect me. He never made me feel less capable than that grandson he never had.*

She heard her grandfather's voice speaking out from the past—"*You've got the world's heaviest pendulum swinging your way, Briar Rose. For pity's sake, take advantage of it.*"

She hadn't known what he meant in those days, but she'd never forgotten his words.

A knock on the door broke Rose from her thoughts.

"Come in" she said, making her hair neat with a brief shake.

The door opened, and Rose drew in a quick breath. As though walking on its own, a spray of blue roses came in, so thick, so wide, so engorged with blooms and leaves that she couldn't even see the face behind them. For a moment she froze. Was the wraith to speak, after all these days?

"Just came for you, Ms. MacKenzie."

The young messenger somehow found her desk and carefully placed the blooming two-dozen at its center.

"Not again..." she whispered.

"Beg pardon, miss?"

"What?" She glanced at the messenger and shook her head. "Who delivered these? Did you see?"

"No, ma'am. But this came with it."

The boy held out his pale hand, and in it there was a glimmer of hope. An envelope. Small, textured, unaddressed except for a single word handwritten on its silvery front. *Rose.*

Slowly, she took it. Her fingers trembled as she opened it. A card. Very simple. Silver-blue. And more handwriting, simple, direct, promise as much as request.

Tonight, in the Simpson Room.

Dine with me.

D.M.

The Simpson Room was a place of heightened mystery for Rose MacKenzie that night. She had arrived at seven, not knowing what "tonight" meant in terms of the clock, but figuring that left the whole evening for the wraith to appear.

"Are you okay?" Phil asked from across the table. "You're sure you don't want me to stay?"

Her wide lips curled in a nervous smile.

"I don't want you to stay," she said.

"It's not too late to have a security guard standing by. And I'm not sure it's such a bad idea, either. Who knows? This guy could be an axe murderer or a serial rapist or, God forbid, a soap opera buff."

Rose couldn't stop the laugh that spilled out over her discomfort with this situation. She looked up at Phil and nodded.

"If he was dangerous, he wouldn't arrange to meet me in the one place in New York where I'm safest, would he?"

"With lunatics, who can tell? Some guys like a challenge. Danger."

Rose shrugged, wishing she'd worn something less revealing than the off-the-shoulder emerald cocktail dress, with its low squared neckline and gathered sleeves that cuffed at her elbows. She was attuned to everything around her, especially the patrons of the dining room beyond her private veranda. She sensed every murmur that moved between the leaves beyond the wall of ferns and palms and begonias.

Phil fiddled with the scalloped edge of the tablecloth. "Rose, I usually tell you the truth as I see it, but— "

"Usually? What do you mean by that?"

With a grin he narrowed his eyees and said, "Just—usually. And this time, I think it's a mistake to meet this guy.

"And why do you think that?"

His grin dropped away. Phil's bright brown eyes flickered from the candles on the table. "Because you've let yourself be captivated."

"Phil," she scolded, "I haven't even met him. How can I be captivated?"

"I'm a lawyer. Lawyers spend half their time figuring out how to get certain reactions out of people. This guy planned it this way. He thought about it for months. He studied you. That's why the roses and the perfume and the note. He's piqued your interest, very effectively, too, and it's a dangerous kind of person who can do that. *I* think, anyway."

Her brows were drawn together, her expression marred by doubt. Rose could feel the tight muscles around her eyes giving her away.

"You think he... studied me?"

"No, it's just a coincidence that your name is Rose, Rose." Phil said impatiently.

"Well, I guess... "

"Would you like for me to sit over there and pretend not to be watching?" he suggested. "Just in case, I mean?"

"I'm a big girl, Phil," she told him. "I don't want to be aware of you. I'll be distracted. Just go back to your office. I'll let you know what happens."

She felt her stomach clench as Aaron appeared suddenly and announced, "*The* gentleman is back in the lobby, ma'am. For the moment," he added with a snap to his voice that said he wouldn't be responsible if the gentleman wasn't there when they looked again.

Rose inhaled slowly. "Show him over."

Phil stood up hesitantly., "Promise you'll call if you need me?"

"I promise. Vanish, will you?"

Good luck, love," he said with a swell of warning in his tone. "And be careful."

In a moment she was alone. Her eyes were fixed on the center of the small table, on the single long-stemmed blue bud that had been delivered to her private table before she'd arrived. The rose sat in a candlelight bath, waiting.

In a corner near the entrance of the Coachman Long Island, safely hidden from the dining room, a tall man briefly surveyed his reflection in the huge mirror across the archway. Did he look as uptight as he felt? He felt like a kid in junior high waiting backstage, about to play opposite the most popular girl in school. But did they have to be playing *Romeo and Juliet*? Couldn't they do a nice quiet comedy or a safe adventure, like maybe *Ben Hur*? Then all he'd have to handle would be a speeding chariot and a few wild horses.

His fingers quivered on his lapel. His hands felt empty, awkward. He didn't know where to put them. He glanced around the indoor foliage for a glimpse of Rose MacKenzie. What was more alluring? Her face? Her hair? Her figure, long and elegant in the sea-green cocktail dress, with the shimmer of diamonds at her throat? She was a work of art, but only because she wasn't like other beautiful women. She was dynamic and genuine, unlike those jaded beauties who pretended to be helpless.

I always thought I could match her. But here I am, finally about to go one-on-one, and all of a sudden I feel like an imposter.

As he watched her from a distance, thoughts he had no business thinking rushed through his head. Confidence, forcefulness, cockiness—would they work to set him apart from other men in her eyes? Would all the years of rehearsing his words and rewriting his speeches and readjusting his image pay off?

"Sir?"

He flinched as the maitre d' materialized beside him. "Yes?"

"Please follow me. Ms. MacKenzie will see you now."

"Ms. Rose MacKenzie... Mr. Daniel Evans Masters."

She watched his approach with unflagging boldness.

Watched every step, every swish of his hands against his stone blue trousers as he strode across the subdued dark green MacKenzie tartan of the dining room carpet, a Viking out of place. The red and gold lines in the tartan sign seemed to reach out to him, grasping the pale gold of his hair and the gentle curves of his cheekbones and shoulders.

She caught a glimpse of the violets, grays, teals, and blues of a patterned sweater beneath the lightweight gabardine jacket he wore, and she had the idea that he wouldn't be wearing the jacket if the Coachman didn't require gentlemen to do so. Suddenly every color in the room had a distinctness that came together in this man who was approaching her. Was it the clothes?

Rose always noticed men's clothes. Maybe it was the clothes.

She had been approached before, many times by many men, but never had it evoked this quiver at the pit of her stomach.

Aaron stepped aside and there was suddenly nothing between them. A sharp, eerie jolt passed through Rose, as though she'd been doused by cool water. He seemed familiar. Did she know him?

She combed her memory. Business acquaintance? No. Perhaps a face from a party, one of those endless affairs she always found some excuse to slip out of? No. She'd never forget that walk of his. From college, maybe? She tried to imagine him in jeans and argyle. No, nothing there either.

High school? She imagined him lankier, at a more awkward time, when boys and girls only dreamed of being men and women, that frustrating time when nothing happened soon enough. No...he wasn't there either.

But there was something, some tiny memory that refused to show itself. She was sure of it. She would find it, though. She would manage to pry up the right stone and he would be there. Because she knew him—she knew him.

If it was only from a story, she was sure she knew him. Thor. Yes. The god of thunder.

A gentle grip embraced her extended hand—somehow she'd found the presence of self to extend her hand. But her gaze remained fixed on his face, the softly freckled features beneath a thick head of cream-blond hair. He towered over Aaron in graceful repose.

Rose had to clear her throat before she could speak.

"Please sit down, Mr. Masters."

"Dan," he said.

And the world fell away.

His voice was a song, a cadence even on the single syllable of his name. Somehow his friendliness cascaded through the mystery.

He slid into the seat Phil had so recently vacated. Curse Phil for his etiquette, anyway; he should have insisted on staying, known that she really didn't want to be alone right now.

"You don't look like an axe murderer," she said abruptly, ramming her thoughts out of the way and taking charge of herself as she had so many times in boardrooms.

He grinned, creating apples on his cheeks that made it seem as though there never had been a mystery attached to this man. "I only swat houseflies," he said.

"Do we know each other?" Rose asked, forcing the issue.

"Do you you think we do?" he responded with what seemed to be practiced evasion.

Rose suddenly felt like a tapestry that had been hanging before him for years.

With a frown, she said, "If so, I don't remember you. Should I?"

"From now on, you will."

"All right," she answered, "let's clear the boards and start again. What can I do for you, Mr. Masters?"

"Dan," he insisted. "You can marry me."

Rose sat back. "Is that all?"

He shrugged, and his eyebrows rose playfully. "For starters."

She tipped her head back, narrowing her eyes. "Is this a joke?"

"I guess it does sound like one, doesn't it?" He smiled at her, with just a touch of sheepishness. So he was human after all. And she had embarrassed him.

Good.

Aaron reappeared. "Will you be dining this evening, ma'am?"

Rose parted her lips to answer, but the voice that sounded was Dan Masters'.

"Of course," he said. "We'll start with caviar canapé with Spanish olives and crab cocktails, abalone soup, and fruit cups. I'll have broiled swordfish with stuffed potato. The lady will have red snapper in caper sauce with heavy cream, and scalloped potatoes. And she likes sprouts on her salad. We'll also be having after-dinner drinks in the Regents' Lounge."

Stunned, Aaron froze in place. Then he pivoted and gave Rose a questioning look.

To Aaron's dismay, Rose managed a nod.

Aaron's eyes widened in horror and he wheeled away, snapping, "Very good, ma'am."

Dan Masters remained stiff-lipped long enough for Aaron to get out of earshot, then he covered his eyes and laughed. "Poor Aaron. I think I'll come in once a week and order sautéed lizard."

Rose continued to stare at him. "He'll be dead in a month. You're either a long-lost brother," she said, "or you've done your research on me. Snapper's my favorite dish. Right down to the heavy cream."

"And the sprouts," Dan said, folding his arms and leaning his elbows on the table. "I know a lot about you, Rose."

"So does anyone who reads a paper once in a while," she retorted. "Who *are* you?"

Like the little guy said: Daniel Evans Masters. That's all I want to be for now...for a while."

"What do you do for a living, Mr. Masters?"

"You mean when I'm not marrying for money?"

Did anyone ever tell you you have the manners of a water buffalo?"

"Oh, yeah."

Rose let her expression fall into complete confusion. She wasn't used to this—sudden appearances by strangers who caused a harmonic vibration deep inside her mind and her memory.

Candlelight flickered on Dan Masters' face, launching lights in his eyes and on his wavy blond hair, and Rose became—for the first time in a long time—conscious of her own appearance.

She compulsively smoothed back a strand of her hair, then inhaled to steady herself. What was he seeing as he looked at her that way?

"I have an idea," she said. "Let's start again. What do you do for a living?"

"Ah," he said. "Okay. Let's say I'm in agriculture."

She leaned forward, determined to match him. "Say a little more."

"Oh, come on, Rose," he said, cupping his large hand over her cool fingers. "You and I both know mystery is the spice of life. If I told you everything about myself, where would the challenge lie?" His wide mouth slanted into a disarming smile.

She didn't blink. "It'll be lying in the gutter beside you if I don't get some details. So far I've got your name and a few piddly flowers."

Dan Masters straightened, drawing his arms away from the table. A pained expression marred his features. "That's how you think of them?"

Guilt smashed through Rose like a solid bolt. "Well...you embarrassed me."

His broad shoulders drooped and his eyes drifted toward the tablecloth. Her words, it seemed, had dashed his hopes—or so it appeared.

"I meant to flatter you," he murmured.

Rose wanted to believe him. But caution reared its head.

Dan continued to gaze down at the table. Then, at last, he raised his eyes to hers. "I wanted to intrigue you."

Rose stared at him, one arched brow rising. There was more to this man than a trail of roses. *Why do I feel there's more between us than a few moments and a few roses?*

She shivered and drew her arms inward, battling with the sensation that he was plunging to the very core of her being, determined to awaken the Rose MacKenzie no one knew, the Rose she had long ago forgotten how to be.

She clutched the linen napkin in her lap and held back the apology that lurked behind her lips. A shot of heat pierced her body when Dan Masters' eyes fell from her face to the softly freckled cleavage over the square-necked dress.

He blinked then, and his gaze lost the intimacy it had taken on for those few seconds.

"I don't know you, Mr. Masters," Rose said, forcing herself to be reasonable. "You don't know me. We're strangers. You've been playing a game with me that I don't appreciate, and I don't have time for. I'd be lying if I said I wasn't flattered and hadn't been intrigued. But please don't do this anymore."

"I do know you," he insisted. "I know you've been trying to learn things with your head that you should learn with your heart."

A strange feeling overcame Rose as this man's words swirled their potent tide around her. She felt bare, found herself wishing she had worn a more conservative dress. Could he look through the rich fabric, right through the warm flesh of her breasts to the very thrusts of her heart? Confusion simmered deep with her, a rising sea of doubts and desires now being stirred by the hand of Daniel Evans Masters—a stranger who knew her.

She swallowed, trying to maintain her composure.

"Let me just say thank-you for the gifts, and let's part friends," she said.

Candlelight glinted on his blond hair as he raised his head and gazed intently at her. She began to wonder what he was really seeing as he looked at her.

"Not friends, Rose," he said softly. "I don't even want to be friends. Whatever it takes and however much it costs...I want to marry you, Rose."

She stood up suddenly, freeing herself from the velvet seat of the chair with a gentle swish.

"Excuse me—" she choked.

She made it to the carpeted steps of the main dining room, but no farther. Dan's fingers closed around the bare flesh of her upper arm and he propelled her back behind a huge potted palm.

Rose's shoulder blades pressed against the cool glass of the window as Dan nudged his body close to hers. He gripped her arms and looked into her eyes with probing intensity.

"You need someone, Rose. You're that kind of woman," he whispered. "Why not marry a man who already loves you?"

He reached up to caress her hair, tracing the line of her jaw, his thumb moving down the strong erratic pulse at her throat. He seemed to be searching for the woman who hid beneath her polished exterior.

Heat rose in her at the sensation of his breath on her lips, and something erupted inside her.

His blond head dipped, and their lips touched...not in cruel passion, not in brutal possessiveness, but in a brushing temptation that was almost a kind of worship, as though their bodies stood in awe of each other. It was simple, pure, physical yet buoyed up by that inner knowledge that this had all begun long ago, in a time that had slipped away.

Her own hands crawled upward against his chest as though to push him away, but the moment her fingers found his heartbeat beneath the cotton sweater the two became one entity.

Then Dan was yanked backward. Rose gasped as a sudden gust of air swept between them.

Rose blinked, backed up—and bumped into Phil. He held her protectively, but his eyes were on the two private security guards who had pulled Dan Masters away.

Dan stood between the guards, off balance, his arms pinned awkwardly back so that his jacket crimped and the sweater bunched up. Mostly, though, it was the hurt in his eyes that Rose stared at.

"Escort him out," Phil said to the guards. "Discreetly, but very firmly."

Dan didn't look away from Rose.

The guards released Dan's arms, let him straighten his jacket, then pulled him away.

Phil coiled an arm around Rose's bare shoulders.

"You okay?" he asked.

She could only nod.

Dan's last words echoed in her mind, drumming, pounding. And the echo hurt.

...a man who already loves you...already loves you...already loves you...

Chapter Three

"I'LL BRING THE car around, Miss MacKenzie."

"Thanks, Tyrone."

Rose stood alone at the curb two nights later, and tried not to appear ill-at-ease on the plush maroon runner as she waited in front of the Coachman. The night air was alive with a cool breeze and the sounds of the city.

New York. A pulse of life without pause. And in New York at night, there was a different purpose in the endless movement of four lanes of buses, taxis, limos, Rolls, Mercedes, and rustbuckets.

Rose inhaled it. She wanted to take the frenetic excitement of the city into her own body and hold it there for a second. The excitement that fed not only the uppercrust, but the millions who worked for them and the millions more who worked for and sold things to the millions who worked. Perpetual motion, somebody had called it. A constantly moving world of living people, all shapes, sizes, colors, brunettes, redheads, blonds...

Blonds.

"Damn," she muttered, clutching her shawl around her. She was thinking about *him* again.

She sighed once, and tried to clear her head.

With a clear head, though, came an acute perception of shadows. There were dark places on the night street, in spite of streetlights and headlights and moonlight. Wedges and shafts of blackness that would serve as hiding places. Even here, in the open, near the curb of a busy New York street, Rose felt suddenly vulnerable.

Of course, she was being watched by the doorman of the Coachman and the security guards, who always looked after her on those rare days or nights when she chose to stand outside.

Was he the type to watch her from the shadows? Certainly he had watched from hidden places, for he knew things about her that a stranger shouldn't know.

He *was* a stranger. She didn't know him.

A man who already loves you.

Only a pathetic dolt would believe a line like that.

So why were her feet cold?

Rose tapped her toe against the carpet impatiently. Her mind replayed the scene in the restaurant, and she didn't like what she saw. Rare were the moments when she wasn't in control, but somehow he had penetrated her defenses. She'd fallen apart, when he gave her that line. She could remember her own starry-eyed reaction, the kind of reaction a teenager would have, which would have been fine if she was a teenager. For a woman her age, there was something disturbing about this feeling. Any other thiry-one-year-old would've laughed in his face.

But Rose's romantic side had never gotten used, so it never grew up. It was still sixteen.

What did he want? Who was he and what did he want?

The most important element in dealing with people was knowing what the other person wanted, what the lines of conquest would be. He'd won round one. It was time for Rose to make up some new rules.

Footsteps.

Rose flinched. A chill engulfed her. She twisted suddenly on the cold street and took a step away from the sound, while staring into the darkness. Someone was coming. Someone tall.

The soft angle of a man's shoulders came through a dusting of moonlight, but his head remained in the the shadows. Then the light was suddenly gone and he was coming at her through a veil of darkness again.

Rose moved closer to the curb. She stole a glance toward the Coachman entrance, but the doorman had chosen this moment to light a cigarette for a woman just going in. Where were the guards?

If she started toward the entrance—she judged the man's approach—they would collide.

The movement in the shadow was right—just the way she remembered Dan Masters' body. She drew in her shoulders and waited for the glint of blond hair and the flicker of blue eyes in the streetlight.

Standing her ground, Rose raised her chin just a bit and glared right at the place where the light would strike his face.

She found herself staring into the dark eyes and bearded face of a Middle Eastern businessman.

She blinked, embarrassed. The man returned her glare with a certain curiosity, then nodded at her and kept walking, his foottaps muffled now by the band of maroon carpet.

"I can't believe I did that," she muttered. She noticed with annoyance that the man was glancing at her again. She grinned idiotically at him as he disappeared into the opposite shadow, continuing down the sidewalk, no doubt wondering who the dizzy redheaded dame was who was talking to herself.

Curiosity began to chew at her. As much as she hoped Dan Masters wouldn't appear, she wanted to look into his face again, with a clear head, to see if the integrity in his eyes had been real or just a trick. The idea nurtured a thrill that Rose couldn't deny.

She had almost managed to get the event in perspective when another clicking noise tapped out from the night. The clackety noise had a certain personality about it, a recognizable cadence and a clear rap that could only go with wooden soles and stacked heels.

"Willoughby," Rose muttered, closing her eyes for a moment. She turned. "Willoughby, how did you know I was here?"

"That's for me to know," answered a ticklestick of feathers and leather that clacked out of the darkness and into the beam of lights from the Coachman's entrance.

The stick materialized into a skinny woman with a black feathered hat nearly covering her short black hair. She walked across the maroon carpet to Rose's side, ignoring the fact that Rose had swiveled away and was glaring down the bustling night street, looking for the limousine. But she was caught. What a pain.

Rose set her lips and turned. There was no escape. "What do you want today, Willoughby?"

Willoughby cocked her own hips inside the tight leather tube she probably called a skirt and responded, "What is this? An attitude?"

"No, no attitude," Rose told her. "I've just had this weird day, that's all. What can I do for you?"

"St. Michael's Children's Burn Unit. What do you think?"

With a mechanical *shuuuush* the Coachman limousine, in all its many feet of bright golden glory, slid to a graceful halt at the curb in front of Rose. Tyrone had maneuvered it so that the VIP door was right in front of Rose.

Rose turned to Willoughby. "I'll have Phil draw up a check in the morning. How much do you want?"

"I'm trying to shake ten thousand out of each of the patrons. We're trying to buy a couple of new treatment bath units, and if you set the pace, everybody else'll have no choice but to come through or lose face. Done?"

Tyrone walked around and opened the door for Rose, knowing full well she could always use an escape from Willoughby Henderson.

Rose stepped into the limousine and settled onto the plush seat. "Ten? That's all?"

Willoughby stepped up to the car and leaned in through the open window. "Are you offering more?"

Rose felt the glow of the entrance lights on her tinted cheeks as she leaned toward Willoughby. "Get the others to match twelve thousand. Tell them I dared them."

"That's the spirit," Willoughby said, fumbling through her purse and extracting a small red notebook. "Twelve grand from the princess. Nice. That's what I like. You have my endless passion and kisses."

"Spare me. How do you keep track of all the charities you sponge for?" Rose asked. "I never how what to expect of you next."

"Next will be saving the seals."

"Willoughby, we already saved the seals. And the dolphins. Most of them anyway. Don't you read the newspapers? Let's go, Tyrone."

"Smart choice, Miss."

"Hey!" Willoughby walked alongside the limousine, tapping on Rose's window with her pen as Tyrone tried to pull out into the tight traffic. "Hey!"

"Just a minute, Tyrone."

"Do I have to?" Tyrone grumbled from the front seat. He pulled the car back against the curb and drew to a halt, then crossed his arms and pulled his cap down over his eyes.

Rose drew the window back down. "What, for pity's sake?"

"What do you mean, what?" Willoughby snapped, skidding to a halt on her stacked heels.

Rose scooted forward on the seat. "Twelve isn't *enough?*"

Willoughby reaaranged herself, spread her hands, and said, "It's Friday."

"Friday?" Rose bolted upright. "Friday! Good God, the auction!"

"Good God, yes."

"I can't believe it's Friday already! All right, get in."

Willoughby grabbed the door handle. Tyrone stretched across the back of the seat in time to push the door open for her. The narrow woman's fringed sleeves slapped in Rose's face as Willoughby stepped into the limousine's wide interior and dragged the door closed behind her. With a twist she landed on the seat across from Rose.

Tyrone pulled smoothly out when he got a break from an obliging taxi driver. Willoughby's streetwise hazel stare cut right through Rose MacKenzie.

"*What?*" Rose finally barked, giving up her unsuccessful interest in the traffic.

"You look," Willoughby began, "like a woman who's having to give up a great evening. Get propositioned or what?"

"No, I didn't. I was just looking forward to a quiet—"

"Like hell you didn't. I know that look. I've had it enough myself. Who is it? John Theolet, right? I *knew* he was after you. Go to bed with him, Rose. You need it."

Rose crossed her legs and tucked her arms deep under her shawl. "I'm not going to bed with John Theolet."

"Oh, why not? He's awesome."

"You're thirty-five years old, Willoughby," Rose pointed out. "Come up with a new adjective."

"You *did* get propositioned."

A nervous grin tugged at Rose's lips. "Okay, all right. I did."

"You turned him down? Who was it?"

"Nobody you know. In fact, nobody I know, either."

Willoughby leaned forward on the seat, her clear hazel eyes

glowing as they stared unwaveringly at Rose. "MacKenzie, listen to mother. Money is great, but it's not a pair of strong arms around you at night. What's a cold bag of coins at your breast instead of a man's hot face?"

Stung by the rock-bottom truth, Rose grimaced. "Willoughby, you're such a yenta."

Willoughby sat back. "Maybe I am," she said with sudden wisdom, "but somebody has rocked the unshakeable Rose MacKenzie."

Rose pressed her lips together and forced herself not to be affected by Willoughby's witchly intuition. After a moment of sublime discomfort, she sighed and asked, "What time is it?"

"Seven-thirty. Not too late to take him up on it." Willoughby leaned back against the velvety seat, pulled a cigarette from her bag and started to light it.

"You light that coffin-nail in my limo and I'll make you eat it," Rose said intolerantly.

Willoughby looked at Rose, looked at the cigarette, then rolled her eyes and stuffed the offensive item back into the bag. "Oh, Christ, I forgot, that's all. All right, level with me. Who was he?"

Rose let her green eyes widen. "Butt out, thank you."

"You've had trouble getting involved with men since you had that fling with Stefan."

"Look," Rose snapped, "Stefan and I had one impulsive, uncomfortable weekend six years ago and that's it. When are you going to quit bringing it up?"

"You mean let it lie?"

"All right, fine. Willoughby, you're taking that so personally and it wasn't personal. You and Stefan didn't even know each other then. It was about as *impersonal* as a fling can get."

"Stefan was infatuated with you. Sometimes I think he still is, Rose."

"Oh, him too? Well, get in line."

"Mmmm...you're hot tonight, Rose."

Rose huffed deprecatingly. "Stefan barely likes me. Kind of how I feel about you right now, Willoughby."

"You couldn't live without a regular dose of me and you know it," Willoughby tossed back.

Rose let silence be her answer. She tried to think of Stefan Henderson, to see his face in her mind, trying to find any lingering feelings, but, just as she had insisted, there were none.

She remained quiet, though her face tightened up in a dead give-away of her perturbing experiences this week. As her eyes began to ache she remembered the strong blue gaze of the man—definitely not Stefan—who had unsettled her beyond all settling, who had said things to her that she would easily have dismissed had they come from anyone else, anyone else without that expression of consummate devotion. Yes, she did remember that. Not a woman who could be easily shaken, Rose knew there was something going on deep beneath the skin, if she could indeed be shaken this much. And there sat Willoughby Henderson, damnably reading her like a book with that unlikely intuition of hers. All this and the auction, too.

"I need a vacation," Rose grumbled.

"Why don't you buy the Bentley?" Willoughby suggested. "Driving around in something like that would be a vacation in itself."

Rose perked up and leaned forward. "Have you been over there? Have you seen it?"

"Oh, God..." Willoughby crossed her arms over her knees and looked wicked. "It's awesome! Sorry—astonishing. It's the best cobalt blue God ever invented, with chrome everythings and even custom-inlaid rosewood trim. It's mint. Not a scratch on it, and Julio tells me that for all he can tell every part is authentic from 1948. The color's not, but everything else is. He's had his guys on it since it came in yesterday, and everything looks perfect. We're able to say in all truth that it's vintage. I can't believe our luck. That car's worth an easy seventy thousand for us. It'll be a real boost for the auction's final dollar figure. And now we have a precedent for demanding that somebody out there make a similar donation of a major item every year. We're going to cure diabetes in this decade, Rose."

Rose gazed at the determined look on Willoughby's intense little face, and suddenly Willoughby didn't look so intense. Behind the powdered complexion and the heavy mascara lurked eyes of pure ferocity, driven not by greed but by the cloying satisfaction of having found her mission in life.

When the Royal Coachman limousine rolled up to the front of the St. James Art Museum, two quite different women stepped out.

Beneath her leather jacket, Willoughby wore a zebra-striped tube dress with a big ceramic toucan pin at her shoulder. The current trends made it easy for funky women like Willoughby, who wore the kind of clothes that worked in casual clubs or formal gatherings.

Rose's dress was more elegant, and far more subdued. Its beaded collar came down into a diamond in front, then broke off into a black silk sheath that fell over her figure with elegance. The sheen of the bronze overdress made her hair look russet instead of red. Her complexion glowed, masking its usual Celtic pale-plus-freckles, and she felt *radiant*.

Even so, Rose didn't outdo Willoughby, who, besides the zebra-striped mini, had on ivory earrings so big it seemed that most of the tusk was still attached.

"Imitation, I hope," Rose murmured as she stood next to Willoughby as Tyrone closed the door behind them.

"Of course," Willoughby said, jiggling her head to make the earrings swing.

Rose surveyed the other woman's clothes critically, then observed, "You have the trashiest taste."

"Jealous," Willoughby swiped. She adjusted her black hair over her ears and stalked past Tyrone to the granite steps of the museum entrance. A marquee battled for attention beside her garish presence. It proclaimed:

GRAND OPENING
CHARITY AUCTION TONIGHT
DONATIONS GOING TO
FOUNDATION FOR DIABETES RESEARCH

Willoughby paused under the marquee. "Come on, Your Majesty. Follow me."

As Rose and Willoughby enetered the old-fashioned foyer of the museum, camera flashes crashed across them and Rose automatically put on her professional smile.

Professional, but she enjoyed this. Enjoyed being treated like some kind of new royalty. People liked looking at and reading about upper echelon businesswomen, and if that made them happy, she was glad to oblige.

What made her *happy* was helping projects like the St. James come into bloom. The small museum planned to display its art in a simple, realistic way. That was Rose's particular influence, a view she shared with Willoughby's husband Stefan, who was curator of this new establishment. They'd once been swept up in a conversation about the tradition of the art museum to display art in a beige vacuum, in big empty halls, on cold stone floors and stolid chalky podiums. Rose loved art, but she hated the uninviting environment of museums. So they would start their own museum: Rose, Stefan, and Willoughby. The carpet would be plush. There would be elegant couches and ottomans on which to rest, lean back, and appreciate the art. The walls would indeed be eggshell, but each painting would be displayed among lovely flowers and carefully arranged standing and hanging plants.

Rose couldn't wait to get inside and see what the designers had done.

"Rose!"

She turned, half expecting to see a Viking striding toward her. Relief spilled into disappointment when Phil appeared from behind the photographers.

"You're late," he said.

"I forgot it was Friday."

His brown eyes narrowed. "That isn't like you. Not with a pet project."

"I know, I know. How's it look inside?"

"Wait till you see it," he said, catching her arm.

"You look great!" she commented, stealing a glance at his double-breasted evening suit.

"Thanks. I knew the suit would match your dress," he told her with a chuckle. "You were right. Garden King did a great job on the floral design."

"I was just thinking about that," she said as he led her inside. Willoughby trailed behind, waving at the photographers. "I hate to pay myself on the back in public—"

"You can this time. I had my doubts about hiring them for a job this delicate, but it sure has worked out well."

"They've always done a beautiful job with the restaurants and and the greenskeeping," she said. "I wanted to be loyal to them—oh! Oh! It's gorgeous!"

From the foyer they stepped into the main lobby, into a world dripping with dark-stained latticework and foliage. All around, elegantly dressed people, strolled through the museum's display rooms, appreciating the decor as much as the artwork. Gentle baby birch trees, compact fig trees, dwarf lilac bushes, and rose topiaries created a fantasy world to walk in, setting a receptive mood even before the first piece of art was glimpsed. English ivy, philodendrons, and sprengeri were everywhere, arranged in wooden hangers and on wooden pedestals. The gentle greens made the whole environment easy on the eye. The colors, which complemented the carpeting and furniture, were adjusted so that none of the plants or floral arrangements drew attention to themselves. They were here to *complement* the artwork, not overshadow it, and the floral designers had nobly kept that in mind.

In the first display room was Rose's personal donation to the cause.

Phil left Rose's side and stepped to the sculpture.

"I never thought you'd part with her," he said.

"Surprise, surprise," Rose murmured, gazing at the bronze casting of an equestrienne riding sidesaddle over a wall. The horse was caught at that perfect moment when a forehoof met the ground again, its hind hooves still hovering over a rock wall, a hound at its side.

The sculpture, worth well over fifteen thousand dollars, had been one of the first in Rose's own private collection.

"When I give a gift, I like to give something personal," she said.

"That's what keeps you from being a snob," Phil said, raising his nose in example.

"I'm a snob," she said, raising her own nose. "I simply hide it with my stunning grace."

They looked at each other for a moment, then broke into laughter. For a moment they were the two gangly kids who used to sneak into Red MacKenzie's Rolls Royce and pretend to be the Duke and Duchess of Windsor.

"You're goofy," Phil commented.

"I know. God, look at everything! I'm so glad they didn't get into anything weird like windswept flower formations. Everything's nice and plain and green. Look how the sculptures show up. I love people who think of things like that. I just love—"

She stopped short, dragging on Phil's arm.

Phil paused. "What?" He looked at her, then in the direction of of her stare. "Goddamn it! How'd *that* get in here?"

In a simple white planter, surrounded by baby's breath and the winking eyes of white lilacs, was a bevy of blue roses. They stood out against the pure green of the other plants with a boldness that was obviously prearranged.

"I didn't see him come in..." Phil craned his neck, looking for that particular face.

"I'll bet he *isn't* here," Rose said, hovering over the blue roses as though she didn't want to turn her back on them. She felt they might get up and follow her. "Men like him don't have the courage. They want to remain wraiths. Mysteries."

"That's what worries me. I'll check before you go into the auction," he said protectively.

She looked up. "No—don't."

"Rose, you don't have to confront him."

"Well, I'd rather confront him than have him lurking around, dropping roses in my path. I want to find out who he is. If I can do that, there won't be anything to be afraid of. Come on. Let's go in."

They entered the auction hall and were greeted with a polite, but exuberant round of applause for Rose as the senior patron of the museum, and Phil as a member of the Board of Directors. From the doorway Rose could see that Willoughby had already threaded her way through to the podium and was standing near Stefan. They were quite a pair. Stefan's neat beard and very English ways contrasted with Willoughby's wild sense of fashion and fun. Yet somehow they looked right together.

Yes, Stefan had once been lured toward the more appropriate Rose MacKenzie, but the chemistry was cold. He had remained cold until stumbling upon the small dark-haired creature who stood with him now. Stefan Henderson was cold no more.

As the applause subsided and Rose and Phil continued into the crowded room toward their reserved seats, Phil murmured, "See him?"

Rose scanned the roomful of her peers, seeking that one face that made anger clash with hope. She didn't find it.

Everything, everyone was beautiful tonight. In spite of the sensation of being haunted, she felt at home. Rose was always pleased to see the many New Yorkers who attended these charity affairs.

People who didn't run in these circles often thought it was competitive snobbery that brought out the socialites with their tuxes and taffeta. Perhaps that was part of it, but Rose spent all her time with these "snobs" and one thing had always been plain to her: no one was more satisfied than the person who just wrote a hefty check to a good cause.

So Rose continued to encourage and to stage these affairs. It had gained her a reputation as a philanthropist, but she still saw herself as the grandkid of Red MacKenzie, the rotund fellow who had once told her, "Rosebud, standing money rots on the vine. Pluck it, and let it be nourishing."

Rose settled into the chair designated for her, in a row with a handful of others who had invested in the museum, at her hounding.

At last, Stefan Henderson raised his long narrow hand for silence.

"Good evening," he began in his heavy voice with its formal English accent. "Without ado, we'll begin our benefit auction for the Foundation for Diabetes Research. We have a charming lineup of items up for bid tonight, all provided to us by private citizens. Tonight we hope to generate a donation we can be proud of for the opening of the St. James Museum. After the auction, we'll be serving a fine table of hors d'oeurves, scones, fresh fruit cups, and tea cakes, as well as champagne and hot beverages in the Eleanor Menzies Room. At that time you'll all have a chance to chat with our wonderful patrons, Mr. Anthony Carrol, Mrs. Louisa del Rizzi, Mr. James Gilver, Mrs. Susan Fisher-Warren, and of course our senior patron and the person largely responsible for the establishment of the museum...Miss Rose MacKenzie."

A round of applause made Rose blush. She nodded her thanks to the crowd, then waved her hand graciously toward the other patrons, who received a second wave of clapping. As she settled back into her chair and the applause subsided, Rose felt warm and in her element, nagged only by a shiver of expectation.

"A generous group," Stefan said with a nod. "Tonight we have an impressive list of items for you to take home in the name of diabetes research. Thomas Lynch, our auctioneer, will detail each item as it is bid. Mr. Lynch...if you would begin please—"

The plump auctioneer, dressed in a white tuxedo, took Stefan's place at the podium and the auction began.

As might be expected, the first items moved rather slowly until people got into the swing of bidding, and suddenly the room dissolved into a friendly bidding war. Rose crossed her ankles and settled back. She felt at home.

And yet...she felt completely alone.

"Sold! For $14,000, to Mr. Kenneth Williams. Thank you *very* much."

Rose had stopped listening a while back, right about the time the penguin pin with the Austrian crystals went for three times its worth. The actual worth of these items didn't mean much tonight. They were just an excuse for people to get out, to show off, to give money to a good cause, and maybe take a little something home from the St. James' Grand Opening. If the St. James survived and thrived, these people would be able to proudly tell their grandchildren they had been there the day the museum opened, and here was this item to prove it.

Rose had hopes like that for the museum, as she had great hopes for many of her little projects. She hoped to help cure diabetes, even though she didn't have it. She hoped to fill premature babies' lungs with the surfactant her corporation was sponsoring, even though she didn't have a baby. None of these things were particularly personal, yet she took them all personally.

Dan Masters had said she didn't let herself think with her heart. As the auction drew to its climax, she knew he had been wrong.

"And now, if you will all turn your attention to the curtain behind me," Stefan began, drawing attention from the auctioneer back to himself, "we give you the showpiece of our kickoff auction, an item so large it barely fit through our loading dock doors. Since it was anonymously donated, we cannot personally thank the generous individuals who provided this premier gift, but they will sleep well tonight knowing how their contribution is appreciated. Ladies and gentlemen...our pride and joy."

As the curtains slid silently back, the crowd gasped and sighed, then showed their approval in a rising warm tide of applause. A shiny 1948 Bentley stood like a prize thoroughbred on parade before them on a wide velvet-draped riser.

Its wide whitewalls and bright wooden trim glowed. Points of light reflected off the chrome and glossy blue paint. The car had a chunky, heavy look about it, its vertical and horizontal lines giving a dignity to its profile. With its wide front end and tapered rear quarters, the classic automobile seemed to be leaning forward, ready to drive away. The applause intensified. Willoughby eventually had to gain the podium and wave for silence.

"Thank you. Isn't it a jewel?" she said, digging for more applause, which she instantly got. She raised a small notecard and began reading from it. "It is a 1948 Farina-Bentley Continental, a two-seater. The interior is gray leather, the dashboard has a polished wood facia panel and precision cockpit dials. This car will go from standstill to 60 mph in twelve point nine seconds. That's almost quick enough for me!"

Laughter rippled through the audience.

"The car has been appraised and insured at today's value, provided by Hemmings Motor News. The insured worth of this classic antique vehicle—" she paused "stands at $64,000."

The audience gasped its appreciation.

Stefan moved to Willoughby's side and leaned toward the mike.

"I had the pleasure," he began, "of driving this car over here, and I can personally tell you it's a thoroughly indulgent motoring experience. Don't be surprised if I take it myself. Mr. Lynch, if you would...we'll begin."

Rose's eyes skimmed over the audience. Someone out there would get the car, and the others would play the game to make the donation a dilly. How much more than $64,000 could they push for? Seven thousand? Ten? She watched as glances flashed around the room. People would dare each other to bid higher and higher. She could already hear the loud buzz at the cocktail party that would follow.

Mr. Lynch took Stefan's place at the podium and raised his hand. "We'll begin the bidding at $65,000."

"Sixty-eight," someone instantly piped up from the back.

"Sixty-eight. Do I hear seventy?"

"Seventy," someone else pushed.

"I have seventy. Do I hear seventy-five?"

"Seventy-five."

The bidder was Ivan Daviston, a bearded man behind Rose on

the left; he was rewarded with polite applause.

"Do I hear eighty?" There was a pause, and Lynch prompted, "Oh, now, we can't let things slow down so soon. Do I hear seventy-seven?"

Rose uncrossed her legs. "Eighty," she said loudly.

Another gasp rippled through the room.

Behind her, Daviston shrugged. "Eighty-two."

"Eighty-two!" Lynch said. "Do I hear eighty-three?"

"Yes," Rose called out.

"Oh, brother," Phil muttered beside her. "That car's going to look damn silly sitting in your penthouse living room."

She smiled, but glanced back at Daviston.

"All right," Lynch chuckled. "Do I hear eighty-four? Mr. Daviston, you want this car?"

Daviston's round body pivoted like a bowling pin, and he tipped his head to each side in contemplation. "Okay, eighty-four."

"How about a nice round number, Miss MacKenzie," Lynch said. "Eighty-five?"

Rose eyed him, her lips closed, and then glanced back at Daviston. How long could they keep it going?

"Okay." Eighty-five," she said crisply.

"Mr. Daviston?"

"Eighty-six."

Phil murmured, "Rose, you don't need that car."

"I don't want it," she murmured back. "Eighty-seven!"

The crowd reeled and turned to Daviston.

But the next bid came not from the rotund banker, but from the back of the room.

"One hundred thousand."

A chill went down Rose's back like frozen lightning. *That* voice.

The crowd turned around at neck-snapping speed, attention turning to the new bidder.

Rose was on her feet and spinning to face the back of the auction room. Stares shifted from the newcomer to her, then back to him.

Mr. Lynch shifted against the podium, and his soft question carried over the sudden quiet.

"Who are *you*, sir?"

Chapter Four

"MAY I HAVE your name?" Lynch's voice carried over the crowd's surprise.

The tall man in back said, "Dan Masters."

"Thank you, Mr. Masters, that's quite a bid."

Masters grinned. "It's quite a car."

The crowd relaxed and chuckled warmly, suddenly receptive to the man whose simple sweater, jeans, and docksiders looked so out of place among the tuxedos and diamonds.

"Oh, I don't believe it," Phil whispered, coming to his feet beside Rose. "How'd he get in?"

"What do you mean, how?" Rose asked quietly, not taking her eyes off Dan Masters.

"I ordered the doors closed as soon as you arrived. I swear he wasn't in here. Do you want me to suggest he leave?"

Rose looked toward the back of the room, making no attempt to disguise the personal nature of the look. She wanted nothing to do with Dan Masters, the man who had made her feel foolish, but there was money flying now, and this was Rose's arena. It was payback time.

"Are you kidding?" Rose said quietly to Phil, though her eyes never left Dan Masters. "I wouldn't miss this for the world. Let it ride." She turned to the podium and called, "One hundred ten thousand."

The crowd reeled again, attention flashing back and forth.

Phil grasped her elbow. "Rose, don't encourage him."

She slowly sat down again, bringing Phil with her, both still supremely aware of the man in the very back of the room. "I'm not encouraging him. He's just here to bother me. Notice he hasn't bid on a single item other than the car. Everything he owns is probably on his back. He's forcing me to fight him, and I'll be he's hoping he loses. He knows I like to win."

How could he know?"

She shrugged. "I don't know. He just knows."

Mr. Lynch touched a folded handkerchief to his forehead and said, "Mr. Masters?"

All eyes shifted to the back. All but Rose's.

Dan Masters stuck his hands in his pockets. "Hundred twenty."

The crowd murmured, but remained rapt.

"Mr. Daviston?"

Daviston perked up from the corner, where he had quickly been forgotten. "No, I'll stick to my moped at that price."

An uncomfortable chuckle ran through the hall, but now everyone was waiting to see what Rose MacKenzie and the handsome stranger would do now that they were head to head.

"Rose..." Phil grumbled.

"I'm going to find out what he's really worth," she said barely above a whisper. "Anyone with that kind of money I'd have heard of by now."

She had to look at him, no matter how she wanted to snub him. She had to see his face. Having dealt in business for most of her life, Rose knew how to judge faces. Slowly she turned.

She watched that face for subtle changes in his eyes, his cheeks, his lips, the muscles of his throat, the set of his shoulders. She had played this kind of poker for millions of dollars at a time, and often before lunch. But from Dan Masters' face she could read nothing, and it frustrated her.

He was as casual and charismatic as a TV minister, yet he evoked a strange curiosity in her, and the feelings he generated within her body had nothing to do with the sacred.

But Dan was looking at her now, and she caught a flicker in his eyes...one tiny flaw in his fortress.

I've got him. He's over his head.

"He's got to be bluffing," she said to herself. "He's got to be."

Lynch nodded at Masters, composed himself, and turned to Rose. "Miss MacKenzie, I have one hundred twenty thousand. Do I hear a challenge?"

"Don't," Phil whispered. "Just call him on it."

Rose took a deep breath. "One hundred twenty-five."

The crowd swelled with response, then held their collective breath and waited, heads swiveling between Rose and Masters.

"Jesus," Phil complained. He folded his arms and sank lower into his chair.

Rose straightened in her chair, not thinking about the fact that she was going to own a small fortune worth of pure spite with four wheels. At least the money would be put to good use.

She smiled at Dan. A smile of victory. He was letting her bid stand. He seemed to have no choice. The lines of his lips had hardened. Rose was sure he couldn't bid any more, and he was losing his edge with the audience.

Lynch cleared his throat. "Mr. Masters? I have one hundred twenty-five thousand dollars. Going once...going twice...and—"

"Two hundred thousand."

The crowd howled, twisting in their seats.

Phil bolted upright in his chair. "What?" He cranked around, as though to look at the words as they flew over the crowd. He covered his eyes with one hand "Jeeezus!"

Rose also turned, gripping her chair, and stared at Dan Masters. He shrugged modestly at the crowd's reaction. She had misread him! Impossible! She was flawless at moments like this, and she hadn't read him right!

"Going once..."

Rage colored Rose's cheeks.

Dan licked his lips, leaned on the wall, and shrugged. It wasn't a fake; it was true modesty. He didn't break his contact with her. They stared at each other over the heads of the audience, lost in their personal tug-of-war. A faint color came up on his face, and Rose couldn't read that either, damn it all, damn it all!

"Going twice...Miss MacKenzie?"

Where was that flicker? Where was that tiny flaw that she had latched onto? Gone, utterly gone was any hint of vacillation on

Dan's part. He gazed at her, undisturbed, as though they stood alone before each other on a silent cliff.

Clack—Lynch brought his gavel down. "Sold! To Mr. Dan Masters for two hundred thousand dollars!"

"What?" Rose gasped.

The crowd whooped and flew into applause for the unknown young man. Several people jumped up and pressed around Dan for a hand-shaking session, thanking him for the fantastic contribution and no doubt asking if they didn't know one another from last year's this or that. Rose knew what the answer would be. No one knew him. He wouldn't have come here if anyone did. That was part of his plan. Somehow she understood that.

Rose choked out, "But I— "

"Don't, Rose," Phil snapped. "Don't—he's got it. The gavel came down. It's down. Don't say anything, do you hear me? Don't talk. Close your mouth."

She forced her jaws together, her lips to stay closed.

"We could make a quiet exit," Phil suggested.

Rose shook herself and took a deep breath.

"Not on your life." Then she added, "How would that look? The senior patron doesn't even congratulate the highest bidder?"

"He's expecting that, you know," Phil said evenly. "He's got to be organized crime. There's no other way he could toss money around like that when no one's ever heard of him before."

Rose watched the covey of people flapping around Dan Masters. "Could be his entire life's savings."

Phil shook his head. "If so, he's dangerously obsessed. I don't think you should go anywhere near him."

She breathed deeply again, feeling her breasts heave against the supple fabric of her gown. For an instant she thought she saw Dan's eyes flash at her from among the crowd.

"You always give me such solid advice," she breathed. "I wish you wouldn't make such sense all the time, I really do."

"Oh? And why not?"

" 'Cause then I wouldn't have such a hard time not taking it."

Phil shook his disapprovingly. "Be careful. That's all I ask."

"I think it'll be all right."

People, like bit players in some kind of dream, fanned out of her way as she moved across the room. Then she was standing near him again. And something about it moved her.

The people watched. The reporters waited. The cameramen focused on her, on him.

"An expensive hello, Mr. Masters," she said quietly. She knew, somehow, that he would hear anything she said no matter how faintly she might whisper it. "On behalf of the St. James, I'd like to thank you for an outstanding contribution to our charity auction."

Dan shrugged modestly and responded, "All in a day's magnanimity."

The people around them laughed and Dan smiled. A flush came up on his cheeks, and he looked strained—or was she imagining it? Was he nervous? Was there a sixteen-year-old in him, too, that perspired as she stood close?

One of the reporters stuck a small microphone toward Dan from between two shoulders. "Where are you from, Mr. Masters?"

He blinked, then looked from Rose to the microphone. "Oh...I've got a little place on the coast."

Evasive again, Rose noticed. Suddenly she was riveted to every word, every nuance of his face, his eyes. Somehow she would get a straight answer out of him.

"Which coast, Mr. Masters?" she asked.

"I'd love to show you," he responded without so much as a pause for breath.

The reporter elbowed his way closer. "What prompted you to overbid to that degree on the car, Mr. Masters? Was it the charity?"

"That," Dan said, "and Miss MacKenzie let it slip before the auction that she'd take the first ride with whoever bought the car. How could I resist?"

"Did you say that, Miss MacKenzie?" the reporter asked.

From behind Rose a familiar voice whispered, "Say the word."

She could've taken Phil up on it, easily. No one would question if she simply said she had other plans, that he'd heard wrong, that she preferred planes, roller skates, anything. But Masters and his charm had the crowd on his side. She thought about refusing, but the words wouldn't come. Besides...

"Yes," she said. "I did say that."

"Are you crazy?" Phil asked with a strange tone of resignation.

As Rose stood near him outside the St. James waiting for Dan and the car to pull up, she had a strange sensation of dejá vu. During the cocktail party Masters had disappeared—big surprise—and magically reappeared some time later, and announcing that the car had been moved out to behind the museum and was ready to roll. Any time, Miss MacKenzie.

A small crowd had come outside with her and Phil to watch her drive off with the Prince Charming who had donated such a chunk for such a car. Funny, nobody mentioned how stupid it was for a woman to allow herself to be driven off by a complete stranger. Dan Masters apparently didn't generate that kind of feeling in people. Something about him made them trust him.

Or maybe they didn't think of Rose MacKenzie as particularly vulnerable.

If only they knew, she thought.

"I'll handle him," she told him, and listened for a note of doubt in her own voice. No, she sounded convinced. Part of her hoped she sounded worried, so Phil would put his foot down and forbid her to go, but she couldn't get that doubt into her tone. When had she lost control?

"You *are* crazy. All I can hope is that his credit is rejected. What's taking them so long anyway? Rose, no one expects you to go with him—you don't really have to."

"*They* expect me to," she said, casting a glance back at the small clutch of patrons and reporters.

"How about if we both go?"

"How would that look?" she countered. "The car only has two seats, Phil. I'd have to sit on your lap."

He smirked. "Doesn't sound so bad to me..."

"Don't worry."

"Why shouldn't I worry? Give me one good reason."

She paused a moment, gazing down the dark street. "Because," she began slowly, "I trust him."

"That's crazy," he said, shaking his head.

"I can't explain it. I've got a sixth sense about people." She held her breath, wondering if he would pick up on the fact that this was the same sixth sense that had failed her utterly inside the auction hall.

"Your sixth sense is tuned in to business, and you know it," Phil said, stalking the curb.

"I just...believe him."

"Believe what?" he asked. "What did he say to you that you have to believe?"

A man who already loves you...

"I'll handle things."

"You said that."

"Phil, you don't understand."

"Don't I?"

She turned. He was looking at her, his gaze crusted with injury.

"Don't I?" he repeated, more quietly this time. He turned away, suddenly conscious of both her and the crowd behind them.

"Oh, Phil—" Rose started to reach out to him.

The crowd began to applaud, and Rose withdrew her hand, confused and self-conscious.

The car pulled up. *The* car.

It gleamed under the street lights in a way it never would in daylight. Its classic lines and tangible aura created a nostalgia for the times of tempestuous starlets and blood-boiling leading men. And there was one of them now—reaching over to push the passenger door open for her.

"So much for his credit being rejected," Phil muttered.

Rose glanced at him sympathetically and started toward the car.

A doorman appeared and pulled the door all the way open. She nodded her thanks and sank onto the supple gray leather.

"Hi," Dan murmured from the driver's seat.

"Hi yourself," she said.

Flashbulbs popped as cameras recorded the moment for the morning newspapers, the tidbit of gossip to go with the morning coffee. Rose offered them a serene smile, covering her feeling of being cornered and wanting to get it over with.

At least there were witnesses. Phil stood on the curb, his mouth tight with disapproval.

It was a good thing someone else was driving, Rose thought. She couldn't have pulled away from him in that moment.

"Where are we going?"

Dan turned the wide black steering wheel smoothly and said,

"We're just going to take a nice long drive. Together."

"I'd rather not," she said.

"Then why'd you promise to come?"

"I never promised to come with you. You backed me into it."

"Pretty well, too, if I do say so myself." His hair feathered over his forehead in the wind.

"It wasn't all that clever."

He glanced at her. "You're here, aren't you? Or maybe you were just looking for an excuse to see me again."

"Don't make any assumptions," she told him. "I don't intimidate easily."

"We'll see."

A chill hit her, enough to drop a silence around them.

And such a silence.

It lasted more than an hour as Dan drove through the glittering towers of New York City and far out into the beautiful tree-lined suburbs of New Jersey.

Rose became overly aware of the sharp, silky click of the gear-change and the weighty precision that had been built into cars of this era. There was nothing in this vehicle for economic consideration, nothing thrifty, no short cuts. The car exacted a steady push against the pavement. Out in front of them the exclusive silver hood ornament and horned bumpers reached for the road.

They were driving through quiet communities on the coast before Dan commented, "Exquisite, isn't it?"

Rose twisted sideways on the wide seat. "Who *are* you?"

The car screeched onto the shoulder and slammed to a stop. Rose instinctively pressed her hand against the dashboard.

The Bentley rocked in place, and settled. Dan shook his head, still gripping the steering wheel. "All right," he muttered. "All right."

He turned in the seat, pulling out his wallet. He opened it and held it before her, his driver's license showing through a plastic cover. With his forefinger he pointed out his name.

"Daniel... Evans... Masters. See the picture? The kind where they beat you up before they take it? That's who I am. I'm starting to hate that question. Here. Look for yourself."

Rose held her breath for a moment, then folded her arms. "I don't want to look in your wallet."

"Are you sure? I mean, it could be forged, you know. Maybe it's Danielle Masters, some poor woman I romanced and killed and erased the l-e' and stuck a bad picture of myself over hers. There's always that. Why do you keep asking me that question?"

"What do you mean, why?" she blurted. "You've got to be kidding."

"I'm not kidding. What would happen if we met on a subway or at a ticket counter, and found we were attracted to each other. What would you demand of me then, Rose? If we liked each other's company, maybe even started to fall in love, would you demand a profile of my past before you allowed yourself to love me? Should *I* ask those things? Should *I* pry suspiciously?"

He pushed out of the car and began pacing the shoulder of the road.

"Then again," he continued contemplatively, "maybe *you* do. Is this how you treat everybody, Rose? With that edge of distrust in your voice? Do you use your beauty and your seductiveness to disarm them and then put them on the defensive with that disbelief? Is that how you make people want to do business with you? Do you make them feel like snakes so they'll do anything and everything you want so they can stop feeling like snakes? Are you so pompous that you think you know everyone who has more than a hundred dollars to his name? Do you really think you're that important?"

She watched him, burying the regret that she hadn't been quick enough to look at the address on the license while he was showing it to her. She got out and stood with the Bentley between them.

"Look who's talking. You've had me on the defensive all along, and I have no idea why."

"I told you why."

"You want to marry me, yes, I remember. I don't think we have to detail the absurdity of that."

"What's absurd about it?"

"The same thing that's absurd about spending two hundred thousand dollars so you can smirk at me. That's a pretty expensive date, even for me."

"I had no choice."

"What?"

"I had to get the car."

"The *car*?"

"The car, the car," he blustered, pointing at the wide blue hood it lay stretched out innocently between them. "The car."

"What are you talking about?"

"I had to get the car back."

Rose narrowed her eyes.

"Back?" she spat. "Wait a minute. Are you trying to tell me that *you* donated this car? And then bought it *back*? I don't believe it."

He spread his hands. "What else is new?"

"I can have it checked out, you know."

"Fine. Check."

"You threw away two hundred thousand dollars just to get me to take a drive with you?"

"That's what it took."

"Phil was right," she said. "You're dangerously obsessed."

He shrugged. "Okay. So I'm obsessed."

"Just like that? 'Okay?' That's all you have to say?"

He paused, his hands in his pockets. His mouth slanted into a disarming grin, creasing his eyes and cheeks with smile lines, but he wasn't really in a smiling mood.

"What do you want me to say? Tell me. I'll say it."

Rose sucked in a hot breath and told him, "I don't want to hear anything you have to say. You can't impress me anymore. I know your pattern now."

His smile dropped away, his mood changed almost audibly.

A cool breeze swept between them, swirling around Dan like a caress. He started moving toward her.

As surely as iron straps, his eyes held her—she was helpless to back away from his approach. She pressed against the door of the Bentley, thoughts of running going through her mind, but she knew from his face that she couldn't escape. She had enveloped herself in this scene and now she would have to play it out.

"Why not give love a chance, Rose?" he asked in a low voice, coming closer, never blinking. "It may prove more satisfying than a contract."

Her cheeks colored and her eyes narrowed into slits, but Rose couldn't move. She was held as tightly as a butterfly in a web, fluttering the wings that once had carried her out of situations like this.

But she had never been in a sitaution like this before.

She frowned at him, her face tight with the haunting feeling that he had looked into her very soul.

"What should I tell you?" Dan asked, his breath hot on her cheek. He grasped her arms and pressed her against the car, until his thighs touched against her legs. "I should tell you I love you, but I already have. I should tell you that I don't have some dark motive, but you won't believe me. All that's left to tell you," he said, his voice dropping to a scorching whisper, "is that you're a woman worth an obsession. And I've paid the price."

Her voice quivered as she tried to retrieve her self-possession. "You've got a lot of nerve, I'll give you that. I've never met anyone quite as self-convinced."

"Maybe it's time you did," he shot back. "Maybe it's time you met an equal. Maybe it's time you *loved* an equal."

He kissed her—dared to do the one thing that would offend her, the one thing he had burned to do since first tasting her lips in the restaurant. But that time she'd been surprised. This time she wasn't.

His mouth cupped hers, covering her lips and sending a volt of delirium through him that he hadn't even anticipated. It *was* the forbidden fruit, it *was* the taste of all time.

A few more seconds, only that...

Rose pulled back, ending the kiss with a gasp of indignation. She glared at him. Dan searched her face during that fleeting moment, sifting through all the nuances that can show on a woman's features, but he found no indication that maybe he had moved her, changed her.

It must be there—surely she must be moved in *some* way, even if she just hated him with more passion! Anything would be better than this indifference.

Green flames roared in Rose MacKenzie's eyes. "And maybe it's time you learned who you're dealing with."

She held her hand up and moved it back and forth once, then again.

Dan turned. A Cadillac and a Chrysler pulled off the dirt shoulder near a greenhouse a few hundred yards behind them. Satisfaction filled Rose as she watched, not the cars, but Dan Masters' face as the Cadillac roared toward them, then braked not ten feet away, the Chrysler drawing up beside it.

Dan stepped back from her. The Cadillac's doors flew open, and Phil Van Dyke and Tyrone got out. From the Chrysler came two men, bodyguards.

Phil stepped up to Rose, the bodyguards moved to flank Dan in case he decided to make a move, and Tyrone opened the Cadillac's rear door.

"Goodbye, Mr. Masters," Rose said, enjoying her moment. "We won't be seeing each other again."

"I think I've heard that before," Dan roared.

She whirled around. "Well, you're not going to hear it again. Save your act for the bimbos, because you're no match for me."

His anger plunged across his eyes, and she loved watching it rush through him.

He lunged forward against the bodyguards' grips on his arms. "Want to make a corporate wager on that, President MacKenzie?"

"Any day, any time, anywhere!"

"Rose," Phil admonished.

"No surprise coming from somebody with a company vault for a hope chest!" Dan shouted, dragging the bodyguards across the center line.

"That's what you think?" she shrieked.

"That's what I think!"

She snapped her arm in rage, giving Phil a yank. "Oooh, just let me *scratch* him— "

"Rose!" Phil grabbed her wrist and found himself being pulled toward the Bentley, until he dug in and pulled Back. "Rose, cut it out!"

"Okay!" Dan shouted. "I'm leaving."

"And I'm supposed to care?" Rose shouted back, tossing her head so violently that her red hair flopped into her face. "Leave! What do you think I've wanted all along!"

"You don't know what you want."

"Just because you're not on the list!"

"You *would* keep a list!" Dan threw off the bodyguards and stalked back to his Bentley.

Phil started pulling Rose toward the Cadillac.

Dan refused to look back as he climbed into his car. The vintage car swung off the shoulder and sped off down the road.

Rose glared at the disappearing Bentley, then whirled and stepped into the Cadillac. A moment later, Phil was beside her and Tyrone was pulling away.

She had won. Or had she? She had seen his face and all the feeling behind it. In spite of her anger, she had seen his eyes—she still saw them.

"You sane now?" Phil asked.

Rose shrugged one shoulder and nodded. Her throat was tight. "How do I have a contract put out on somebody?"

Phil shook his head. "You have to admire the guy. He's clever and he's got nerve." He glanced back through the rear window. "I think he got the message this time, though. You won't have to see him again."

Staring into the back of the driver's seat, Rose fixed her eyes on the blank gray leather and searched her heart for the feeling of victory she had expected to have at this moment. It wasn't there. When she spoke, her voice held neither joy nor triumph.

"Then why do I feel this way?"

Chapter Five

"I DON'T CARE what it takes or costs or who it annoys. I want to know what he's up to."

"Up to, okay."

"This isn't fun anymore. He's hiding something, something big. He can't have that much money and not be traceable. And you know...sometimes, in the right light, he *does* look familiar to me. Don't glare at me that way, Phil. Pull in some favors. I want to know what his angle is. Put Hendricks on it."

"How do you know he's got an angle?"

"You think something else?"

"Well, I think he might—"

"He's trying to blindside me so I don't see him coming from another direction. He'll come out of nowhere and knock my knees out if I don't head him off. Get McCall's nitpicky secretary to run down all the classic car organizations around. Clubs, too.

"McCall, got it."

"Check the colleges in the area for alumni records."

"You can't get confidential information just like that, Rose."

"You can if you pay enough."

"Oh...right."

"Have you checked on those blue roses yet?"

Phil sighed. "I'm checking. It's not that easy. There are some lavender roses and some silver ones registered with the American Rose Society and some other rose specialists, and they told me there *is* in fact a blue rose, but the name of the hybridizers are kept confidential. The Society told me I have to try contacting the blue rose people by mail, through a post office box. I guess sometimes these flower people get kind of eccentric."

"Tell me about it!" Rose stopped pacing.

"Then ask the police to help. Tell him he's harassing me or something. And call that Templeton woman from the League of Women Voters. She owes me a few, God knows."

"Yes, she does..."

"He's funneling me for a fall, I can feel it."

Phil looked up. "Why would he do that?"

"Who knows? Maybe he's got a grudge. Lots of people blame others for their failures."

For the first time in twenty minutes, Rose fell silent. Now only the sound of the car's engine and the hum of tires on the pavement, and the scratch of Phil's pen as he jotted down her instructions made any dent in the tension. They drove back to New York and she went up to her apartment under a sudden pall.

She should've asked Phil to come up with her, so she wouldn't have had to be alone right then. Once the business Rose had had her say, the private Rose was a little lost.

Why was she so angry?

Simple. Because Dan had won.

What did he want?

And why did she feel...abandoned?

Oh, this was crazy...*crazy*.

She contined to feel that way. That odd, uncomfortable, unfinished way. She didn't know him, despite the confidence in his voice. As safe as she was in the privacy of her own secure penthouse, she was still haunted. Yet she found herself imagining what he would look like with the golden rays of the sun sliding over his wavy blond hair, darkening his Bahama-gold tan, warming the strong muscles of his shoulders and thighs.

Rose was a woman who hated to admit weakness in herself, but she'd learned over the years that even *that* was a weakness. She had learned to admit being wrong. Maybe this was one of those times when her prideful, bombastic personality had to take a back seat, when her competitive senses had to bow out.

As she fixed herself a cup of hot chocolate, she tired to shake away Dan's image. But the more she fought, the stronger the image became. Firm cheekbones, a subtle jawline, gilt hair, and a half-grinning mouth below those penetrating eyes.

Rose, his voice floated in her mind, *you're going to marry me. I can give you the excitement you crave and the love you want.*

Had he even said those words? Or had his eyes only spoken? Why was her mind answering?

Want your love? How do you know what I want? What have I forgotten that you're trying to remind me of? Why do I feel there's more between us than a couple of short meetings?

She tried to be angry, but even the anger was falling second to a strange penetrating desire.

He's gotten under my skin, she thought as she stirred the hot chocolate. *He bothers, me that's all. And I'm sitting here wishing for more. Maybe all I need is a good vacation. Time to clear my head.*

But the image refused to fade. It continued to hover in her mind...

Dan standing there, his hands casually hidden in his pockets, as he waited for her to walk to him...

That was it—that was the damning part. In spite of his forwardness, he was making her want to come to him. Somehow he was doing that!

She tried to get some sleep, but halfway through the night a restful sleep was tumbled by haloed visions of a tall blond god of thunder, one whose eyes were the buds of tiny blue roses, whose hands felt like the touch of velvety petals, whose voice was as captivating as the sound of wind through roses. The voice said she would never be satisfied to simply follow the set trail her life had been taking. There would have to be more. He would show her. There *could* be more.

She saw lips she hungered for. Once again the contours of his body were pressed against the woman within her. She awakened in a pool of perspiration and need.

It was three-thirty in the morning, but sleep was now impossible. She got up and made a pot of tea and a sandwich, but those too failed to ease her.

With the mug of tea in hand and her silk pajamas flowing from her shoulders, Rose wandered around her penthouse, looking at her collection of sculptures. She preferred the perfect duplication of life—even in fantasy. Porcelains by Cybis, Goebel, Laslo Ispanki, Lladro, bronzes, by Bugatti and Obarra, and fine reproductions of classics by Michelangelo and Rodin. A few rare or antique pieces were encased in glass, but for the most part the collection was out and touchable. Rose loved to reach for a drink on one of her tables and have her hand brush against the more-than-human perfection of a Cybis American Indian or an Ispanki princess strolling through some fantasy garden, or the wing of a sculpted eagle so lifelike her guests shied away in startlement.

She had tried her hand at sculpture in college, desperately hoping, but her hands wanted nothing to do with it. No matter what she sculpted, it turned out to be an owl. An ambitious owl, occasionally, but still an owl.

She loved good pieces all the more, and found great solace in lovingly handling them when she was disturbed.

Her enchanted world was failing her now. She had built her own prison and decorated it with frozen echoes of life. Her finest moments were locked in illusion. She hadn't begun to live yet.

When the phone rang, she barely heard it. It rang again, and she blinked.

Who could be calling at this hour?

She glanced at the brass clock. Almost four. Finally she went over to the round black designer phone.

"Hello?"

"Morning, Rose. Were you sleeping?"

She inhaled sharply. Emotions crashed through her mind. She was about to slam the receiver down into the cradle when she saw something from the corner of her eye. She turned. And kept the receiver at her ear as her eyes fell on the replica of Bernini's *Apollo and Daphne.*

The young god was frozen in a run, his hand just folding around the soft white belly of the nymph he adored, a child on the verge of womanhood, who feared his love so much that she chose to live out her life without love at all—in the form of a laurel tree.

"At four in the morning?" she said, then fell silent.

Poor Apollo. It was just dawning on his face that he'd lost her. Her legs were being encased in rising bark, her hair and fingers elongating into leafy branches of laurel, a tree he would later make sacred in memory of her. Sympathy lanced through Rose as she listened to the silence on the other end of the line, as she looked at Daphne's supple legs hardening into wood and the pain of realization on the boy-god's face. Rose could almost hear his heart pounding. He only wanted to love her. Why was she so afraid.

Dan's voice broke the silence. "Are you there?"

Rose blinked. "Yes. I guess I'm here."

"Thanks," he said quietly. "You can't sleep, can you?"

She wasn't surprised that he knew.

"Neither can I," he said, without waiting for her to answer. "I'd like to come over, Rose. I'd like a chance to apologize. We need to talk...a little more." He paused. When she said nothing, he finally asked, "Would you clear your building's security for me?"

No, no, no.

Her eyes turned to Apollo and Daphne.

She whispered, "Yes."

When the doorbell rang, she jumped. Chimes went off in her chest as she hurried to open the door.

Dan's chin was tipped downward in something like shyness or candor. He was dressed even more casually than the last time she'd seen him, this time wearing slacks and a plain charcoal denim shirt. The sleeves were rolled up above the wrists and the collar open to reveal a tuft of blond curls on his chest. His hands, of course, were buried in his hip pockets, making bulges.

"Hi," he said.

"Hi," Rose responded, gesturing him inside.

He hesitated, seemed almost unwilling to make that commitment to come in. Yet Rose got the distinct feeling there would be no closing the door in his face. His mellowness didn't diminish the sense of determination he carried with him.

"Would you like something to drink?" she asked as he wandered to her shellbacked chair, but did not sit.

"Yes, matter of fact, I would."

"Do you like Irish Cream?"

"Yes, I do."

She went to the curved marble bar, filled two glasses with the cordial, and joined Dan near the backless channel-quilted couch in the center of the large living room.

"How did you know I was up at this obscene hour?" she asked.

He took the glass she offered. "I don't know. I just had a feeling you wouldn't be able to dismiss me with a swipe of a hand. So I took a chance and phoned. I really didn't think you'd let me come up..."

"I didn't think I would either," she admitted. "You could be a midnight slasher, for all I know."

"Then why did you let me come?" he asked.

She shrugged one shoulder. "I'm not sure. Maybe I'm as curious as I am foolhardy."

Dan sat down, leaning against the high curved end of the sofa. "Were you surprised to hear from me?"

Rose couldn't resist a smile, if a small one.

"No. I would've been surprised if I *hadn't* heard from you. You're not the kind of man who gives up."

His face took on an evocative brightness, and he smiled cagily. "Would you respect a man who gave up, Rose?"

"I don't know," she said. "I haven't met anybody like that lately."

Dan gazed intently at her for a moment, then glanced around her apartment, taking in the predawn warth. After a moment he rose, too wired to sit beside her.

Slowly he paced the room. He took in the hardwood floors and the elegant furnishings, and one by one he examined the sculptures.

Try as she might, though, Rose couldn't tell what he was thinking. Were these luxuries familiar to him? Was he used to tossing hundreds of thousands of dollars around, or had he indeed made a fling of his life's savings in order to impress her? She repressed the thought of Phil's offhand suggestion of organized crime.

"I'd like to know more about you," she said at last.

"And I you," he tossed back.

"Don't be evasive," she challenged. "You already know more about me than you have any business knowing. I don't particularly like being an open book to someone when I didn't supply the information."

He signed. "You make me feel like a KGB agent."

"And you make me feel like a portfolio that suddenly fell open on the floor."

"I know," he murmured, and sipped his drink. His long lean body shifted gracefully as he rocked on his heels, hand still stuck in a pocket. "I know. That's why I'm here right now. I don't want you to be afraid of me, Rose. You probably realize by now that this is more than just a lark for me, more than just the intrigue of seeing if I could get into your life. Whatever you've meant to other men, you mean much more to me."

"That wouldn't sound like such a come-on," she said, "if we'd known each other more than a few days."

"I know."

He went to the glass doors that led to the rooftop garden, gazing at the vast green panorama beyond the glass. Clumps of flowers caught the moonlight and the glow from inside.

"This is great," he said. "A garden as dynamic as you are."

Rose wondered if he was still avoiding the subject, or if he was looking for a suitable place to bare his soul.

"Would you like to see it?" she asked.

He stepped aside, and she opened the double doors, ushering him into the penthouse garden that owned a piece of the sky.

The stars above New York were dimmed by the vast glow of a city without sleep, but night's blanket gave the beauty of jewels to endless city lights. Here was Rose's version of New York's many skyscraper-top forests and Dan took it all in. Green hedges surrounded clusters of impatiens, rows of marigolds, phlox, and geraniums. The air was perfumed with their fragrance.

"Hmmmm," Dan said, inahling and looking thoughtful, "I smell thyme. And— "

"And lily-of-the-valley and— "

"No, don't tell me." He held out one hand, then breathed again, turning where he stood. "Lavender... verbena, mint... jasmine, right?" He turned back and gave her a long, bewitching gaze. "And roses."

He made his point with his eyes, the kind of point that can't be caught or worded, but only felt in some deep chasm between hearts.

Rose shifted uneasily.

Dan broke the spell, moving deeper into the garden. On the other side of a brick-lined raised bed, Dan found a little clutch of rattan chairs, a table, even a hammock hidden in an area cloistered by a vine-covered trellis with hanging ferns. Small pots of petunias and scarlet sage dotted the redwood deck, muted by the moon. There was even an old wrought iron fountain gurgling in a shaded corner, with a large goldfish flitting in its moonlit tub.

"Not bad," Dan said.

Rose approached him. "Not bad?"

"It lacks a certain…wildness that I like."

"I love it out here," she said, an edge to her voice. "I sometimes stay out here all night."

Moonlight glinted on his pale hair. "Camping?"

"I don't have to worry about bears, so why not?"

He moved close to her, too close. "You see? We have a lot in common."

"Do we?"

"I love to camp in the woods."

"This isn't quite the woods—"

"I've been known to take off for some uncharted forest for weeks on end. I've learned to appreciate the beauty of camping alone." He touched the fronds of a thick ladyfern. "After a while, I even quit telling people about it."

"You're telling *me* about it," she said.

Suddenly his face was ablaze. "You need someone to tell you about things like that. Otherwise you'll turn into one of these potted plants, always growing inside a little round restriction, never being what you can be, and that," he rasped, "would be a tragedy."

She watched him under the moonlight and the harsher light of the city. He took a step toward her.

"Would you come to the forest with me sometime, Rose? Soon?" he asked softly.

She dared a little laugh, trying for haughtiness. "Just like that?"

He hovered there, several paces away. In the dimness, surrounded on three sides by manicured tiers of flowers, he resembled an attorney making an impassioned case before a jury of pansies. The flowers nodded their little faces in a breeze from the nearby sky. "Please don't sound so threatened. I really don't mean to threaten you."

Every instinct told her to believe him. To believe that he didn't want to hurt or frighten her.

"I didn't mean to sound that way," Rose admitted. "What did you have in mind?"

"Time alone. You and me. Anywhere but New York."

"What are the stipulations?"

As soon as she spoke, she knew she'd made a mistake. She could tell from the way he shook his head.

"Rose, Rose... always business. I can almost see the cogs turning inside your head. You've let yourself be devoured by Red MacKenzie's legacy. It's given you everything, but it's hammering your heart into a little safety deposit box. It's bad enough when that happens to a man, much less a... woman."

He shook his head again sadly, then stared off into the pink-gray predawn sky. New York was becoming a butterfly rising from the cocoon of night.

Dan sighed and strode off a pace or two. "I don't know who came up with the idea that having brains has to kill sensitivity in a woman, but I wish they'd trash it." His hand disappeared into a fern and he fondled it. "You're like the furniture in your apartment—cool, stylish, severe... maybe even a little static. But to the touch of an appreciative man, you can still be soft and receiving."

He turned slowly, as though he knew what his body was doing to her.

"Please invite that touch, Rose," he said, "before you become something that's only for looking at."

A single beam of moonlight broke through the hanging plants above, to kiss Dan's blond hair, shining on his words, as though it had been trying to tell her the same thing for years.

Nervous, Rose murmured, "What do you want from me?"

"I want a week of your time. Just you and me. We're not corporations. We're people. We could be special to each other. It's only a week... but it's plenty of time to salvage the woman in you. Rose—listen to me. Is this the voice of a man who's lying? Give me one week. If I can't convince you to love me in those seven little days, I'll go away. You'll never see me again."

Trembling, Rose drifted away from him, across the deck toward the fountain, determined not to let him cloud her mind.

She couldn't clear her head. His words were so soothing now, so full of personal needs and promises, reaching out to caress her in a way that made her think of his hands and his arms, his body, his eyes. Almost hypnotic, these words, a poetry she would at another time have nodded at and dismissed.

She made herself look back at him. She saw a dark man-shaped outline, a shoud of pre-dawn sky as its corona. She stared helplessly into the shadowy area of his face, unable to see the features.

"What...what do you get out of this?"

Dan stepped closer—but only one step. A gentle, slow step that swelled before her. When he spoke, the words were so simple they couldn't have been hiding a lie.

"I get the chance," he said, "to love you."

He took a step, then another, playing the short distance between them like a musical instrument.

"Rose," he repeated, playing her name, "give me the chance to love you."

She trembled and took a step backward. "Who are you?" she whispered. "I have to know, Dan. I know we've been together before—I *know* we have. That's why I let you come up here. We know each other—I'm sure of it. Tell me."

"Yes, we have been together before," he said. "A long, long time ago. But I won't tell you yet. You have to love me because of what you feel, not what you know. You can't marry a pile of dates and details."

"Stop talking that way," she gasped.

"Why? Somewhere in you there must be an echo of impulse left...something must be left of wanting love for love's sake."

Rose inhaled slowly, caught the scent of Irish Cream on his breath. "I can't be irrational..."

"I *want* you to be," he said. "And I want to be the human element in your life."

Rose's throat tightened at the sincerity in his tone. She shivered. She battled with the feeling that he was plunging to her very core, determined to awaken a Rose MacKenzie no one knew, the Rose she had long ago suppressed. Intense intimacy passed between the two of them as though she had indeed known him all her life after all. She began to shrink away. He would have none of it. For every quivering step she took away from him, he closed the distance between them by twice that.

Perhaps he saw the answer in her eyes, and was waiting for it to burst from her lips. She could taste it lingering there, ready to evaporate if she dared speak. She denied the confusion that simmered keep inside, desires now being stirred by Dan Masters as he reached for her, caught her.

His words ebbed in her mind like the foam of a strong drink, spilling over to soak the soil in which a tiny nameless seedling grew. She felt bare, and wished to be wearing more than silk pajamas.

How does he know?

His voice folded around the two of them with a sensual power as he spoke.

"You've been trying to make a decision with your head that you should be making with your heart."

A wave of vulnerability swept over Rose as Dan's fingers gently closed around her upper arms. She thought his touch would sever them. He slowly pressed her against one of the open double glass doors. With probing intensity he looked deep into her eyes. His hand slipped up to caress her hair, then traced the line of her jaw, his thumb moving down over the strong erotic pulses of her throat. She knew he could feel the heat rise in her body at the sound of his voice as he spoke one final time.

He murmured, "I want to be the argument of the heart."

Anguish erupted within Rose. It was pure, simple, physical, yet buoyed up by that inner suspense.

Too much acceptance...too much of his body pressing against hers...too much response along the pathways of sensation, her very flesh calling for more from him, more of him. Humiliation slid into desire. It would have been perfect to die beneath the questing of his lips, letting all her embarrassment tumble away, while giving her the chance to dive headlong into what he offered.

Her hands moved up his warm pounding chest. The kiss became hungrier, moister, and gradually became the intrusion he hadn't meant it to be.

I want to be the argument of the heart.

And she began to struggle.

Chapter Six

THE PAVEMENT WAS cool. It still held the chill from last night, and that chill seeped through the seat of his pants. He was as numb to it as to the warmth of the morning sun coming between the skyscrapers.

He sat on the steps of the building next to hers. It was as far as he had gotten.

Echoes of his behavior up there in the sky with Rose now thundered in, feeding a headache. I want, I want, I want. How many sentences had he started that way? Why had he held her so tightly?

He pressed his hands against his temples, but the echo wouldn't stop. People in business clothes stepped by him, but no one stopped, no one spoke.

New Yorkers rustled by him, on their way to their day. He was aware of the curious glances, but they meant nothing to him. His face was unshaven, hollow from lack of sleep, his shirt considerably more rumpled than it had been when he'd first appeared at Rose's door. With the heels of his hands crushed against his temples, he probably looked like a drunk just waking up on the pavement.

She'd shocked him, and he was worried. Not yet afraid of failing in his quest, but getting there. She wasn't the little girl he thought she'd be.

She had ripened. She was sophisticated. Maybe she knew what she wanted more than he had anticipated. Any other woman would have melted—he knew, he'd had enough of them. He'd felt the rising tremors in her body that matched those in his, but she hadn't given in to him. She hadn't buckled.

Was he going to get his week alone with her? He didn't know.

Even if he did, how could he tell her truth? He could say, "Rose, this is who I am and this is how we're tied together, and if I don't marry you, I lose everything I've worked for—"

That'd be the end of of it for sure.

Maybe he should just consult another lawyer.

And get the same answer. Again.

He folded his hands and pressed his lips against them as though to seal in the rude way he'd spoken to her, all the mistakes he'd made that he had told himself he wasn't going to make again. It was all catching up with him now—Rose, the past, the tomorrows.

For a moment he took stock of himself. Looks. Okay, he wasn't bad to look at for a minute or two, but he'd been born with those. Money. That had been work, but that was okay. He knew as well as Rose did what had to be done to get more and more of it. But that didn't put him in the same league as Rose MacKenzie. That didn't make his body, corded with muscles born of hard work, good enough to rub against the scented softness of her powdered skin. She wouldn't want the real Dan Masters, with dirt blackening his fingernails and slivers in his palms from the shovel handles.

She had probably thought he was trying to seduce her with that kiss. Couldn't he have been able to control himself? But the moment he touched her, out flew the clumsy boy. Unwanted images of himself flooded the tortured brain thumping between his hands. Here he sat like a summerstock actor after a botched performance. Forgotten lines, uncued entrances, and an audience that deserved better.

He raised his aching eyes to the tip of the building next door. The urge to rush up there and apologize to her was overwhelming. He sketched it all out in his mind. He'd stumble off the elevator and sink into the richness of her company, stammer his sorries, rattle off the truth about his past and what he was doing now, and beg her to forgive the rogue who kept taking over.

He imagined her drifting through the penthouse garden, totally out of reach. He remembered again how she'd schooled him. He'd found himself outside the apartment, hearing the door clicking closed behind him, hearing his own rashness echo in his ears, and wondering how he'd let himself end up outside of her life again.

She hadn't thrown him out. She'd *gotten* him out. Gracefully, like wine flowing. All at once, womanhood jumped two rungs on his ladder of respect. Here was a real woman, that being floating around up there, out of reach.

He put one foot on the sidewalk, paused, then pulled it back. All he needed right now was to make matters worse by trying to explain what he'd gone there once to explain and already screwed up.

"Ass," he mumbled to the shadow beneath him. "Yeah, you."

"Masters?"

At the sound of his name, he blinked into the bright sunlight and focused on the sheen of a brown three-piece suit, a briefcase and a paper cup.

Dan shaded his eyes.

"Oh...hi."

"What are you doing here?" Phil Van Dyke asked, not moving closer. He had stood there for several seconds already, before deciding that this cement-step recluse was indeed the impeccable Dan himself. After a moment he gestured upward with the briefcase. "Were you up...?"

Shifting self-consciously, Dan shrugged. "For a while."

He stopped squinting into the bright light and leaned foward with his elbows on his knees. His stomach was cramping from too many hours with nothing to work on but a few sips of Irish Cream. He hoped Van Dyke would just walk away. He didn't like being seen this way.

The shadow of the other man moved and, in fact, came closer.

Phil paused a moment, then leaned slightly, trying to see Dan's face. Slowly he asked, "You all right?"

Dan looked up, straightened his back a fraction, and tried to tug some of the rumples out of his untucked shirt.

"That bad?" he asked.

His surprise redoubled when Rose MacKenzie's attorney sat down on the step beside him and handed him his cup of coffee.

"Here."

Phil held the coffee between them, hoping Dan would take it, as a gesture of acquaintance if nothing else. It had smelled so good as he passed the street vendor a block down. Dan looked like he needed it.

"Thanks," Dan said. The aromatic steam coiled around his face and brought color to his cheeks.

Setting his briefcase down on the step, Phil hiked his trouser legs up and bent his knees. "Did you spend the night? No—don't answer that. It's none of my business."

Dan squinted at him. "You don't trust me."

"It's not up to me," Phil said instantly. "I only keep out the riffraff."

Dan arched his brows and scanned the busy street.

"Well, I guess I can take that as a compliment." He sipped the coffee, not in a hurry to speak again. "Are you still digging into my mysterious past?"

"How'd you know about that?"

"Walls have ears, counselor."

"Hmmm." Phil sighed. "Rest assured, I haven't found anything yet."

"You won't. I've made sure of that."

"Don't be *too* sure of it. Money like hers can buy a lot of information."

"Well...there's a flip side. Money can buy a lot of false turns."

"Maybe," Phil said quietly. "But I'm betting it's not your money. It's a smoke screen of some kind."

Dan shrugged one shoulder and clasped his hands as his elbows rested on his knees. "Whatever makes you happy."

Phil looked at him cannily. "Is Rose okay?"

"You mean, did I leave her a ravaged lump of sobbing flesh on the floor while I strode away saying, 'Frankly my dear, I don't give a damn'?"

Phil took his turn at embarrassment, and raised a white flag in his tone. "Sorry."

Dan stared at the pavement for a long moment. Making a decision, he grasped the handrail and climbed stiffly to his feet, bothered by his own clumsiness.

"No...listen. *I'm* sorry. I don't blame you for protecting her. I'd protect her too."

Phil nodded slowly. "I do protect her," he said, "and I intend to keep on protecting her."

"From me?"

"Yes. If you're out to hurt Rose, I'll find out about it."

"Then what?"

"Then," Phil said, "I'll have to use it to ruin you."

"I see."

"Maybe you do. Maybe you don't, I don't know."

Phil clasped his hands and leaned forward, actually relaxing as he set up the battle lines between them. He met Dan Masters' gaze without the slightest flinch.

"I don't know who you are or what you want, but I'm going to know soon."

"Yeah," Dan grunted. "So will everybody."

"If you've got some kind of a scheme going to use Rose," Phil continued, "be forewarned. I'm not going to let it happen. I've been protecting her too long to let you slip by."

Dan shruggged, watching Phil's face for the tiny changes that would signal the undercurrents of intent. Clearly they were men of the same mettle, even if one was the hunter and one the hunted. The outcome would depend on how well the environment was handled.

Dan's gaze suddenly sharpened. For a moment he had seen something else. A perception so profound that Dan tossed away all the typical threat lines such men often bandied and went for the soft underside—honest intuition.

"You love her, don't you?"

Phil blinked, but his expression remained under control. It was no secret. He'd never really tried to make it one. Even if he had, he would've given himself away each time he glanced at her, each time he paused before answering her and had to shake himself out of the hypnotism she evoked.

"Some day she's going to turn to me," he said quietly, looking Dan squarely in the eye.

"No, she won't," Dan said. "I'm here now."

Phil took a deep breath and let it out slowly.

"That's pretty wild."

"It's wild," Dan admitted. "You're wrong for her. That's why you're down here and she's up there."

Phil's dark eyes flashed in the bright sunlight reflected off the pavement. Tiny lines of annoyance creased his features. Coolly, and correctly, he pointed out, "You're down here, too."

The traffic made a humming noise in front of them, curling around Phil's words, enhancing their damnable accuracy.

"You're right," Dan said. He dismissed the tension with a small chuckle. "I guess I am. We'll see who stays down in the end."

He got up, his legs aching, his buttocks like solid wood from the concrete steps. He turned to Phil.

"Thanks for the coffee... it was damned civil of you."

He searched his pockets as Phil watched.

"Do me a favor, will you? And I don't blame you if you won't—" Lying in Dan's palm was a tiny blue rosebud, crying of delicacy and meaning. "I didn't get to give this to her."

For a long moment the two men—in many ways the antithesis of one another—stood on the stone steps.

Phil looked long and hard into the fatigued eyes of Dan Masters. Then he opened his hand and reached for the rosebud.

Chapter Seven

A DAY—AND a night—later, a vintage airplane rumbled its low song over the open grasses surrounding the airstrip. Rose approached the old plane as she had a thousand times, but this particular time she was reminded not of her grandfather, but of another vintage vehicle and the man who called it his own. Another man, a very different man.

The chunky 1939 Douglas DC-3 was war-surplus, a pet of Red MacKenzie's, purchased just after the war, customized at great expense, re-christened *Briar Rose*, and put on the payroll of the MacKenzie Foundation. Formerly a 28-seat heavy transport, the plane now sported a plush interior divided into separate salons.

She climbed the gangway and walked into the plush main salon, which was more like a living room thatn the interior of a plane.

Four swiveling lounges locked into place for take-off and landings, a polished wood foldout table, and a neatly arranged entertainment center on one wall. There was even a tidy galley with all the trimmings.

Phil sat in one of the lounges, calm and steady as ever, waiting for her.

"I'm late, I know," Rose said as she settled into the lounge across from him. "When I got up, I found your message on my machine to meet you here, but I have no idea where we're going. Where *are* we going?"

Phil chuckled. He gazed into his open briefcase, pretending to be wrapped up in the day's business. He blinked as he saw the tiny blue rosebud lying inside the briefcase, waiting to be given to her. He paused, then quickly, but guiltily, covered the rosebud with a pad of paper.

"We're going to the new site," he said. "Dallas."

"Right. Dallas. I'm ready."

Phil smiled, hoping she didn't pick up on the guilty tint on his cheeks. "You don't look ready."

"Where is everybody today?" Rose asked.

"I assume Grant's in the cockpit as usual," Phil said. "The plane was running when I got here. And I gave Louise the day off."

"Why? Do you like to serve your own food?"

"No," he said. "I just had a feeling you might like to have a private kind of day."

Color bloomed under Rose's faint freckles.

She nervously adjusted the neck of her cream-colored cotton dress and kicked off her shoes. "All right, you caught me."

"Rough night?"

"A little."

"You want to talk about it?"

"I'm trying not to think about it."

"Why, Rose?"

She looked at him suddenly now, though a second ago she had been trying to avoid his eyes. Phil gazed back at her, and knew his expression was betraying him.

Rose leaned forward. "You know, don't you? You know he was with me."

Phil's breath caught in his throat. Did she know she looked like that? Did she know she was an artist's dream in this light?

That golden light danced on her sleek hair and creamy complexion, and in the green of her eyes? Her face was unadorned.

There was a faint tint on her bare shoulders, as though the sun had reached down from the sky and kissed them. Was this how Dan Masters had seen her last night?

A trickle of sweat ran down the middle of his back. Today he might be losing her—if he had ever had her at all.

"Phil?" she asked. "What's the matter?"

"Nothing," he blurted. "Just thinking."

"Then answer me."

"Rose, it's none of my business. I'm not comfortable discussing him with you, please."

"Does that mean no listening, too?"

He sighed. "No, of course not. I'm sorry. Go ahead."

Rose settled back in the chair, her tall frame giving shape to the simple dress, her hair and eyes giving it color where there was none. She gazed out the plane's small window and felt the rumble of the engines coming up even through the plush tangerine carpet. Through the window she saw the plane's 30-foot wing arching over the runway.

"It was like being in Neverland, Phil. It was fantasy. I almost lost control."

"What's wrong with a little fantasy?"

Rose's mind cluttered with answers, but the real one was tucked away in a hidden pocket of Dan Masters' spy cloak. "Only that I'm afraid of it. I'm afraid I can't handle it. I never realized how much I needed the control. I thought I had a grip on all my weaknesses. God...running the whole corporation is easier than this."

"What does he want?"

"He wants me to go away with him for a while. Away from New York, away from everything."

"And what do *you* want, Rose?"

The question caught her by surprise. It was the simplest and most logical one, but somehow it hadn't occurred to her. Now it rang in her head. What did she want?

Memory and anticipation clawed for front row seats. The wanting ...needing—these were the real sexual act, the true eruption. The body ached, the legs trembled, the heart wept a tune of joyful need. Wanting, as potent as the having. She'd had lovers before. Sex was easy.

But no man had ever made her *want.*

Why wasn't he here? He was always around before. Why wasn't he here now?

"I don't know what I want," she murmured at last.

The seatbelt light started blinking, and Rose was saved from saying any more.

She and Phil dutifully—and gratefully—turned their lounges to the proper forward position, locked them in, and buckled their seat belts. In moments they were airborne.

The sensation of being away from the earth came as a startling relief—away from New York, away from Dan, away from having to make a decision right now. Another city, other things to think about, work to concentrate upon—that's what she needed. But as she gazed out the window, she found herself wandering in a garden of blue roses. She bent to pluck one, but their serrated leaves quivered on long thorny stem. The rose turned its cool blue lips up to mock hers. Blue eyes, obstinate, unremitting, refused to release her from their spell.

She had no idea how long she stared out the window. Far below, the pattern of the Earth changed. The city was gone; there were trees. Mountains. A different world.

"Rose?"

She flinched.

"Sorry," Phil said. He was standing over her now. "Were you asleep?"

"No...no, just thinking."

"Mind if I go forward and give Grant a break at the controls? I feel like piloting for a while."

Rose pushed the images of flowers from her mind. "Okay, have fun," she murmured. "I always feel secure when you're at the stick."

"Sure," Phil said. "Never mind Grant's ten billion flight hours."

Sitting forward, Rose stretched her shoulders. "Let me know if you two get hungry. I've always wanted to be a stewardess."

"What kind of a stewardess would you be?"

"Fly the plane."

"You can't even make a good rum and Coke."

"*Fly* the plane!"

Now that he had gotten her to smile, Phil felt better about abandoning her to the solitude. The flight cabin door opened, then closed behind him.

She was alone. All alone.

She turned back to the window. Once again time became fluid and she lost track of how much of it flowed away—until she felt a faint weight drop into her lap. Instinctively she looked down...

She stared at the splash of blue and green lying bright against the cream of her dress. The blue rose of her dreams. Here. Now.

"Hello, Rose."

She tensed and her cheeks flushed at the sound of the provocative voice buttering over her. She spun the lounge toward the center of the plane. There he was.

"I don't believe it!" As Rose bolted to her feet, the rose tumbled from her lap.

Dan stooped gracefully and picked up the discarded rose, holding it like a lost child.

"I don't believe it!" she repeated, taking a step backward. "You were...you've been...all this time? Where's Grant!"

"I gave him the week off."

"You did what?"

Dan just smiled at her.

"*You* were piloting the plane?"

He shrugged, his blond head tipping casually. "Well, I *can* do it—I spent a few years in the Air Force. I've been flying since I was nineteen."

Rose stared at him, her shoulders slumping suddenly.

"You are incredible," she breathed. "How do you do these things? How did you get my pilot to leave?"

"Call it my near-magical salesmanship and personal flair. Smart people trust me automatically."

"Do they?" She tossed her head, her silky red hair bouncing against her neck.

Dan stifled an urge to reach out, to touch her hair, her skin. Only regret about last night's performance kept him from it. Until he knew what damage he'd done, there would be no more reaching out.

"I could apologize," he offered, "but I'm not really sorry. I guess I could apologize for not being sorry. Would that help?"

"You know, if we weren't twenty thousand feet up," Rose said, "I'd push you out of the plane! But that'd probably do you more damage than even I want," she concluded. "God, you should get a prize for all this. In fact, I'll give you one. One that you deserve."

Dan's bright eyes grew even brighter. "Oh?"

"Yes."

"What?"

"I'm firing Grant."

His expression changed instantly. "Rose, don't. It isn't Grant's fault."

"Isn't it? How can I trust a pilot who lets a stranger take over my private plane?"

"Rose, please. I lied to him, I conned him. I told him the trip was postponed."

He caught her hand as she settled into her chair once again, and to her surprise he hunched down there beside her.

"Please?"

She put on her coldest expression. She had no intention of firing Grant; if she did, she'd have to fire herself too because she'd also been fooled. But how much would Dan allow another man to be punished for his own brashness? This she wanted to know.

She straightened her spine and did what she did best. "Sorry. I have to be able to trust my people."

Dan's jaw locked, his lips pressing into a hard line. He stood up, dropping her hand like a rock. Stuffing his hands into his pockets, he strode the length of the cabin and back.

"All right, fire him," he said, his voice rough. "I'll hire him myself. My God, you can be a block of rock sometimes, Rose."

Her icy glare washed over him. "People have to pay for their mistakes, Dan. That's how it is."

The cabin lights cast a flat light on Dan's blond hair and a faint shadow over his eyes.

"Yes," he said. "Maybe I'm making one right now." He dropped into a lounge and swiveled away from her, trapped into this situation by his own relentlessness.

Rose sat quietly, thinking. Maybe he really wasn't as self-concerned as he'd seemed at first. He really was concerned about Grant. Hmmm…

She'd won the upper hand, struck the hardest blow, as she knew so well how to do. Without taking her eyes off his lounge, Rose quietly asked, "What did you have in mind for your week with me?"

The plane rumbled around them, slipping through the daylight sky, the only sounds for what seemed like hours.

When he finally spoke, his voice was stiff with resentment and disappointment, disappointment in her, she knew.

"I could don a bolero and woo you with romantic ballads from below your balcony, but your balcony is sixty stories up and I'd need some killer heel lifts for that."

"All right, all right." She felt the sting of his sarcasm, and she even smiled. "I won't fire him, okay?"

Rose listened for a response. There was one, a faint sigh. Of relief?

She turned her lounge toward his. "Where are you from? New York?"

"Nowhere," he said. Then he too pivoted his chair, and they were facing each other over the polished wood table. "No, I'm not being evasive. I was born in Youngstown, Ohio. My mother died when I was eight. Dad was a military man, so we moved a lot. I've lived in a dozen towns in the States, and Europe. Germany, Belgium, Scotland— "

"Scotland?" Rose perked up at this sudden reminder of her beloved grandfather waving from her reverie. "I love Scotland! My Gran used to take me there almost every year. I haven't been back for a long time."

Dan's eyes smiled. "I love it too. I love old places."

"Where are you from now?"

"I have a cottage in Connecticut and an apartment in New York."

"Not that I could find," Rose put in saucily. "And this cottage is home?"

"It's the closest I've ever had to having a home."

"And family?"

"I have a family. Brothers and sisters, two of each."

"Five of you?" Rose's eyes widened. "Seems unlikely for a military man who moved around a lot."

A cloud passed over Dan's face, and for a moment Rose thought she'd said the wrong thing.

My mother never fully recovered after my youngest sister was born," Dan said. "Dad still thinks the doctor screwed up, and to this day he hates hospitals. She died a few months later and he kept shuttling around the world, with all five of us in tow. We're scattered all over the world now. As we traveled, each of us picked up his or her own interests and settled wherever those interests rooted. My brother Wayne is an Egyptologist for a major museum in London. My other brother is a realtor in California. Big sister Eleanor's a news correspondent in South Africa, of all places. She's nuts, but she's happy."

"And the other one?"

"Anna. In college, I think her major this week is musicology. As for Dad," he added, "he's still trying to outrun the memories."

Rose leaned forward in empathy, the soft cotton jersey of her halter dress cupping her breasts. "Oh, Dan, that's so sad! He must have loved her very much."

"Yes. Because we all watched him go through it, we got to know the effect one person can have on another. It affected us different ways. Eleanor's the oldest, and I think she was too close to the pain—I doubt she'll every marry. Anna, on the other hand, only saw the lasting love in Dad's eyes and she was mystified that love could sustain itself. I think she understood him better than all of us. Whenever we were groaning about having to move again, she'd by clinging to Dad's leg, telling him it was all right and that he was doing a good thing. What a kid..."

"Do you see her very often?"

"Oh, sure. For a scattered family, we see each other a lot. I guess the ties were magnified because we were all we had. No home, no friends, just each other. We know what it's like to lose a precious limb."

Rose gazed at him sympathetically. "You sound like my grandfather." She waved a hand around the cabin. "This plane is named for my grandmother."

"And so are you," Dan said quietly. "Was she as special as you are, Rose?"

Rose cast him a small, spontaneous smile just before she glanced away. As he caught sight of the tip of her tongue moving behind gleaming teeth and glossed lips, a thrust of arousal hit Dan's loins so strongly he nearly moaned out loud.

He tried to stay away from her, to avoid making the same foolish errors her desirability had pushed him to make on that lonely night in her penthouse, but he could only hold back so long. His hand moved out toward her. His body followed, cupping her hand with his. He slid from the seat and stretched his body out along hers, not resting against her, yet. His hand slid up the softness of her arm, savoring the sensation of bare skin. Her legs were warm against his muslin trousers. Only the mightiest of effort capped the urge to explore them.

Sensing that he was holding back, Rose was torn between relief and the need to soothe his reluctance. The smell of him, the sight of him, the feel of his body resting softly against hers all seemed overwhelmingly right.

She couldn't help but respond to it.

Dan's lips were near hers by now. He touched her elbow, caressing the delicate bones, finding the sensitive spots as though he knew them from long ago. He made no rough moves, vowing to stay gentle, to hold off the savagery that rattled at the base of his being.

Rose let her eyes drift shut at the first touch of his lips on hers. Her jaw slackened, and she was lost in him.

It was a soft search for contour and sensation, but Rose could tell that he was holding back. Why?

This unexplained reserve worried her, but also intrigued her. She was drawn closer even as he bridled himself, as though he was somehow opening himself to her trust by making her follow him through that uncertainty. Her heart jumped as his palm pressed her ribcage beneath her breast. The warm open feeling of his kiss dragged her along. The monumental tenderness he offered. The purity itself was arousing.

"Dan," she whispered.

Dan drew a breath suddenly, then pulled away so quickly he almost fell. They separated and he stumbled to his feet, breathing heavily.

"I know, I know. I'm doing it again...I can't help it, Rose. You don't know what you do to me."

Rose stood up and moved toward him. "That was the most civilized behavior I've seen from you yet."

"Oh, no," he chuckled, "I'm not civilized. I'm a barbarian. The kind who'll muscle you to the floor and drag you away by the hair."

He turned away from her and put his hands on the galley shelf, as though to restrain himself.

"What is all this?" Rose demanded. "I've never gotten such mixed signals from anybody before. What do you want? Do you want to kiss me, or not?"

"What, another deal?" he snapped.

"Dan, what do you *want*?" Rose asked reasonably. "You keep

forcing these confrontations, then it seems you don't know what you want from them. I always plan— "

She stopped herself, but it was too late.

He snapped around. "A meeting?"

For lack of a more appealing image, she simply said, "Yes," even as he stood there watching her silently.

Her green eyes sparkling, Rose rested her long hands on her hips and surveyed him with the critical eye of a woman who knew how to read people.

"I haven't figured you out yet," she said, "but I will."

For an instant she saw a faint vulnerability in his eyes, but, then it was gone, like a firefly in the night, and he was impenetrable again. His eyes again took on an iron will.

He sighed suddenly, and the hardness washed out of him.

"I'm tired of this," he said. "I can't keep it up anymore."

"Well, finally," she snapped, not expecting to really hear anything at all.

But there was something different about him this time, in his posture, in his expression. He stared out the little window as though into the past.

Then he started to talk.

"It was a long time ago. We were both just teenagers. You were just starting to act as hostess at the Coachman Long Island. A prerequisite to taking over, I guess. You were so pretty...but, boy, were you skinny!"

A quiver ran down Rose's spine. She didn't dare move.

"You would usher people to their tables," he went on. "And I would watch you through the big windows overlooking the putting green. I worked as a greenskeeper— "

"You!"

Rose shot out of her chair.

"You! That boy! The boy with the knobby shoulders and the sun-streaked hair who was always looking at me! It was you!"

She laughed as though she'd just discovered buried treasure.

"That's where I met you! You're Danny the Hedgeclipper!"

Dan blushed and shuddered. "Oh, God...I didn't think anybody remembered that nickname...why did *you* have to?"

"*That's* your big secret?" Rose wailed. "Why didn't you tell me!"

He laughed. "Because I was afraid you'd remember that goddamned nickname!"

Rose swatted him playfully. "You've put me through all this, and all the time you're Danny the Hedge— "

"Don't say it again," he begged, holding up his hand. He caught her by the wrists and murmured, "I had such a crush on you then... I thought it'd come through my chest and kill me."

Rose gazed at him, memory swelling with the picture of a narrow youth with a sun-streaked mop of hair that hung over his eyes in sweaty strings. At sixteen she'd given up noticing the surreptitious glances of the young gardener from outside the high windows. She'd learned that puppy love was fickle, and other interests had pulled her away.

"I wasn't in your league," he said. "I knew I wasn't good enough for you. I didn't give you enough credit to give me a chance."

"You left all of a sudden," Rose remembered. "I looked out that window for weeks... but you were gone."

"I didn't know you looked. I went away. I couldn't stand the pain in my chest anymore. I worked to become good enough for you. What a jerk I was... at first I didn't trust you to love me because I was poor, then I didn't trust you to love me because I was rich."

Rose shook her head.

"You... that was you... you've really changed!"

"Can't have changed that much," he said innocently. You recognized something about me."

"Enough to drive me batty!" she said. "I can't believe it. That's all there is to all this mystery?"

"Well," he said softly, "I won't say I don't have other secrets."

"At least I know I'm not losing my mind!"

They stood together gazing into each other's eyes for the first time without the pane glass separating them. Relief poured through Rose like spring water.

When tragedy struck, they were still in another dimension.

The old DC-3 canted suddenly to one side then righted itself abruptly, but not before both Dan and Rose were cast sideways. They landed in a tangle in one of the lounge chairs. Rose gasped. She was crushed under him, but this time there was no warmth in it.

Dan rolled off her and staggered to the porthole.

A loud thud on the outer hull of the plane was soon followed by several more thuds. Then the thudding became like rain on a tin roof, and the aircraft began to shudder.

"What the hell—" What he saw made him gasp out loud. "Oh, my God!"

Rose tried to pull herself up in the chair. Just then the cabin door swung open.

"Dan!" Phil called. "Need some help!" His voice cracked.

Dan stumbled to the cockpit. As rose lurched through the rolling plane after him, she caught a glimpse of him dropping into the copilot's seat.

"Geese!" Phil choked. "Hundreds of them! I came out of the clouds into them."

"Can we climb?"

"Not anymore. Look at the engines."

Rose pulled herself into the cockpit behind the two men, sucking in her breath at what she saw.

Streaks of blood and feathers spattered the windshield. Beyond the stains, dozens and dozens of white-feathered bodies made an eerie cloud all around them, clogging the engines, damaging the propellers. It was like a scene from a grotesque horror film.

"Oh, God!" she shouted. "Get over them!"

"We can't." Dan coolly surveyed the old-fashioned dials in front of him. "She won't climb anymore."

The engines, clogged with mutilated birds, cracked and started to roar as though in pain. Bent propellers no longer turned with their usual even hum, rattling and clacking unevenly.

"Rose, go back and strap yourself in," Dan ordered in a carefully controlled voice.

"I don't want to leave you," she said, trembling.

He darted her a quick glance, and a smile. "Finally!"

She glared at him, but Phil turned and said, "He's right, Rose. Do what he says." His knuckles were white, and the color had drained from his face. "You can't help. You'll be in more danger if you stay here. Go strap in."

Rose stared at him. "Are we crashing, Phil?"

"Please, Rose."

Rose would rather have pulled her own teeth than leave that

cockpit, but she knew it was foolish to stay. She backed out on quaking legs, watching the men's shoulders flex with effort. At once she had a vision so strong it nearly floored her.

She could lose them both.

Dazed, her eyes went from Dan to Phil and back again in total confusion.

Dan was working the controls, Phil was barking their location into a crackling radio, and all around them the plane was whining and groaning, roaring and tilting.

Phil's voice seemed to echo. "Mayday...mayday..."

Trees shot by beneath them. Loss of altitude—that must be it...Rose trembled so hard she could barely breathe. A crashing corporation she could handle, but a crashing plane?

Outside, the plane's porthole, mountainous country dropped off with terrible abruptness. The engines sputtered. Rose heard one engine die, its propeller moaning sluggishly, losing power.

Rose's hand crept out before her, yearning to touch the solidity of Dan's shoulder, seeking the tremors that came with touching him, as though they could reassure her.

"Can't I stay? Can't I help somehow?" she asked.

"Get going, Rose!" Dan roared suddenly over the shriek of the engines.

His order pierced her, making her jump. She retreated and strapped herself into a seat as far foward in the salon as possible. The next minutes were a blur. Rose sat alone, unable to help, frightened by the coughing of the damaged engines. The plane twisted and tilted as trees shot by the windows. Were they that low? Why was the sun shining? Branches cracked outside as the plane sliced through the tress. A wing strained and then smashed against something solid. The whole aircraft yanked around like an ice skater being spun.

Rose screamed, but it was cut off as she was thrown forward against her seat belt so violently her nose hit her knee.

The cabin was jolted. Everything that wasn't tied down crashed forward into the firewall. Metal shrieked as it was peeled from the plane's structure. Trees cracked and glass shattered as the plane continued to dive belly-down into a stand of trees.

The port wing broke entirely then—Rose actually felt it crack off—and an ugly black shape crashed through the plane's hull, crossed in front of her. She pushed back in the chair and screamed again.

The fuselage shifted foward and sideways, and creaked to a halt.

Silence dropped in, uninvited.

Glass tinkled. Electricity snapped like bacon frying.

Boughs moaned outside. A bird cried his outrage at the intrusion, then flew away.

Chapter Eight

A LOOSE DOCUMENT on the hiring of a new maitre d' at the Coachman Copenhagen drifted and curled in the air, then skidded to a stop on the leaf-strewn carpet. A leprosy of scattered articles cluttered the deck of the tilted plane. The silence was worse than the crashing.

Rose pulled her hands back from her hot face, feeling as though each section of her body had been detached from the rest. Her eyes misted over, but the tears would not fall. She found herself staring at the rough bark of the tree limb that had pierced the side of the plane.

Another foot, and it would've killed her.

Killed...

She listened intently for a sound from there. Had she lost one of them? Both?

She tugged at the buckle of her seat belt, her hands trembling and cold. At last the belt fell away from her hips.

She pushed away from the tree limb and tried to stand up.

The condition of the plane shocked her. Most of the windows were broken. A breeze whistled by overhead, which frightened her because she knew she shouldn't be able to hear it all. The fuselage must be cracked...open. The sun intruded in patches. She looked up.

"Rose!"

She whirled and fell into Dan's arms as he crawled from the cockpit. "Oh, Dan!"

He held her tightly against his chest, clinging to her, stroking her hair for a moment. Then he put her away from him.

"Where's the first-aid kit?"

Her mind flashed aft to the galley and forward to the cockpit in the same instant.

"My God!" she shrieked. "Phil!"

Dan held her back as she tried to push by him. Only the stability in his eyes and voice allowed Roes to hold off the panic.

"Get the first-aid kit, Rose," he said steadily, syllable by syllable, calming her. "Open the main door and let the air clear. Then get some clean towels and come forward."

He squeezed her shoulders.

With a nod, she scrambled toward the galley. Rose seized the medikit and towels, carrying them as though they were weapons, as she moved toward the main door. A moment later, she had pushed it open on its massive hinges.

She wasn't prepared for what she found in the cockpit. A tree branch as thick as Dan's body had broken through the windshield, smashing the control panel. What had been a windshield was now open air framed by jagged glass. Rose gasped when she saw that and again when she looked at Phil.

Dan was bent over him. Phil was moving slightly. A hand-sized piece of glass protruded from the hollow of his shoulder.

"Phil!" Rose whispered jaggedly.

'Dan was packing off the wound with a handkerchief, taking great care not to disturb the glass itself. He took some gauze pads from Rose as she stood there, uselessly.

"Did you get the door open?"

Rose could only stare at Phil.

"Rose!"

"Yes! Yes, I opened it..."

"I'm going to take him outside. You get a pillow and blankets. I want him out of here until we're sure there's not going to be a fire. Do you understand?"

"Yes."

"Go on then."

Tears streaked Roses's face, but she did as she was told.

Her arms full of blankets and pillows, Rose climbed out of the plane into the mountain wilderness. The territory was lush with ferns and an endless carpet of moss and timberland. Shimmering sunlight offered only cold comfort.

The smell of moss twined through the odor of leaking fuel and oil confused Rose's senses as she searched for an open spot on which to lay the blankets she was carrying. Finally she chose a knoll a safe distance from the broken hulk of the *Briar Rose*. Neither war nor Red MacKenzie's rough handling had been too much for the old plane, but here she was, sundered by a hapless flock of geese.

Rose began to realize that danger is never where you could expect it to be.

Dan appeared at the main port, pulling Phil out after him. Rose ran to them, but other than helping support Phil, there was nothing she could do. She touched Phil's damp face and mumbled words of reassurance. She hardly knew what she was saying to him. The glaze over his brown eyes frightened her, but he did squeeze back when she gripped his hand.

"Let me support his weight," Dan said. "Don't let him work too hard. Take it easy, Phil. I've got you."

He seemed to know what to do, so Rose was content to let him do it.

"Slowly," Dan said with effort as they lowered him down. In a moment Phil was rolling onto the makeshift bed. "Got the towels?"

Her hands so cold she couldn't feel them, Rose nodded.

"Fold one and put it under his head. Give me the other one to put under that shoulder."

Dan shook out the towel she gave him and rolled it lengthwise, then carefully raised Phil's injured side and placed the towel under the bad shoulder. He leaned over the other man and asked, "Phil, can you hear me?"

Phil moaned, digested the words, then managed a small nod.

"You'll be okay, I promise," Dan told him, "Try to relax as much as you can." He lowered his voice then and drew Rose close to him. "When I take the glass out," he said into her ear, "you put those pressure packs on. Think you can?"

Rose clenched her fists, then picked up a stack of gauze pads. "I can," she said.

Dan carefully gripped the piece of glass and levered the shard out with one smooth movement.

Phil came alive with pain and dug his fingernails into Dan's arm. Dan let him claw as much as he needed to and held him down. Rose let instinct tell her how much pressure to apply. But she was hurting Phil...oh, she was hurting him so much...

Phil grimaced and turned paper white. Dan held onto him. He glanced at Rose. "He's in shock."

"Shouldn't...shouldn't we elevate his legs?" Rose stammered, taking refuge in Dan's blue eyes where she found strength.

"After we stop the bleeding. We don't want to force blood to an open wound. For now just cover him and keep him calm."

Her eyes widened and she nodded and swallowed. With one hand she pulled a blanket around Phil keeping the pressure on his shoulder with the other.

Dan's fingers brushed the hot skin of her throat, drawing her attention back to him. He was studying her face, the wisp of copper hair caught on an eyelash.

"What about you?" he murmured. "Are you all right?"

Rose managed a nod.

"I thought about you while we were coming down," Dan said. "I wanted to be back there holding you—I was afraid I might lose you before I had the chance to have you."

A tendril of hanging moss toyed with the blond waves in his hair. Their eyes exchanged a poignant message, and his words took on a huskiness.

Rose's eyelids drifted closed. She tipped her head into his palm, admitting that those had been her needs as well. A person in mortal danger sees her life pass before her eyes. Rose had seen Dan.

And he had been fading away.

Phil stiffened beneath their hands and drew their attention. Dan caught Phil's hand and kept it from venturing up to his wounded shoulder.

"Phil, listen to me. Look at me."

Phil forced his blurred eyes open and met Dan's steady gaze.

"Don't try to move at all, understand?" Dan told him quietly. "I'm sure we got a clear mayday out, so they'll be looking for us soon. I'll take care of everything, but you've got to rest or you'll sap all your strength."

"Rose..." Phil groaned.

She leaned over him. "I'm here, I'm here."

Her voice seemed to soothe him, and he slipped into unconsciousness.

"Phil!" Rose choked.

Dan leaned over the other man and spoke more firmly. "Phil?"

But Phil no longer moved. His breathing settled down to the nearly inaudible.

Dan watched him for a moment. His own shoulders slumped and he muttered, "Jeez..."

"Oh, God," Rose whispered, "Oh, no—"

"Rose, he's all right," Dan reassured her. "He's just unconscious. Let's immobilize that arm while we have the chance."

The bleeding now under control, they cut off Phil's shirt and taped a pressure bandage into the hollow of his shoulder. Then they wrapped a crude sling around his arm.

Dan draped a wet cloth over Phil's eyes and forehead, then sighed. "That's all we can do for now. We should get some supplies from the plane. Are there flares on board?"

"I don't know," Rose murmured. She forced herself to think. "There has to be some kind of emergency equipment, somewhere in there. Grant knew all those things..."

"And it's my fault he's not here," Dan sighed. "But there's food, and we have our clothes, so..."

His words trailed off as Rose stumbled to her feet and roamed away.

Dan watched as she bumped into a tree and ended up hugging it, her shoulders and arms shaking violently.

He grabbed a blanket and stood up.

Clinging to the tree, Rose wanted to cry, scream, let the fear out, but she, too, was in shock, especially now that the worst was over and she was wading through the aftermath. How did people do it? How was it possible to face disasters and come out sane? Was she strong enough?

She barely noticed when Dan draped the blanket over her shoulders and pulled her around into his arms. Gently he urged her to lay her head against him. His hand skimmed her back and in a moment she was crying. The sound made him feel relieved, and as her panic purged itself, she trembled less and less.

Her hand crept up his chest.

"I was so scared," she whispered through a sob. Terror began to dribble away. "We're lucky you were here..."

Her throat clogged on a sob and she turned her face against Dan's neck. Since her eyes were closed, she never saw the pain in his face.

The fear retreated, but like a caged animal it remained nearby.

Rose was a woman of the city, of concrete and lights, straight streets and buildings. The forest was an alien environment, especially with the chewed-up hulk of *Briar Rose* lying in the stand of trees like a corpse in its grave. The beloved old DC-3 had been a staple in her life, and every time she glanced at it the way it was now she was lanced by her own mortality.

Things could end...abruptly.

As she collected twigs for a fire, Rose tried to think logically. Did she dare let her own pride kill what was building between her and Dan? Was he the type of man who would take a mile if she gave him an inch?

The sun floated across the sky, morning into afternoon, and the shadows began to lengthen. The day slipped by in incongruous peace. Phil was still unconscious. Rose hovered beside him.

Things shouldn't be this quiet, this peaceful, right after a plane crash. There should be sirens. Fire trucks. Lights. Ambulances. Oh, Phil...

Why wasn't he lying in a nice, clean hospital bed instead of a bed of chair cushions, underbrush for a mattress, and wrapped up here in coarse blankets. Where were the reporters? Where were the people who always fussed over them. Why was she here in the woods picking up sticks and hovering over her unconscious best friend?

She straightened and saw her dress. The white jersey was covered with moss and soil, her feet were bare. Not exactly Givenchy, more like Annie Oakley. And her lips felt dry, cracked. No more lip gloss. Maybe there was some in the plane...

As she looked up she saw Dan standing near the plane. He put his hand on the one remaining wing, bowed his head a little, then sank down to kneel in the soft ferns. Even from here Rose could tell that something was wrong.

"Dan!" She dropped the sticks and ran to him.

He looked up as she arrived at his side. His eyes were strained, and he was working to keep control over his expression.

"Dan?" Rose knelt beside him. "Are you hurt?"

He shrugged. "Oh...I guess I slammed my hip on something when we hit."

"Why didn't you say anything?"

He managed a tight smile. "I just did. Look on the bright side. I've probably got a bruise from here to my toes. That kills any particular desire I might have for being seen without clothes."

Rose's brows drew together in empathy. "Oh, Dan, I feel terrible..."

Dan grinned at her lewdly and crooned, "I bet."

"How can you joke about it?"

"I'll prove it. Let me hold you."

Rose shook her head and settled down on the cool ground beside him. "Aren't you something," she murmured.

Dan moved his leg into a better position, but couldn't stifle a sharp wince as he got settled. "Don't look at me like that, Rose. I'm okay."

Rose coiled her arms tightly about herself and looked through the trees to the sky. "When do you think they'll find us?"

"Could be any time. Or any day. It depends on how close we are to the location we gave them in our mayday. But either way, they'll spot us soon. Civil Air Patrol or somebody'll find us."

"Soon enough for Phil?" Rose asked, aware of the edge in her voice, but helpless to hold it back.

Dan sighed and looked across the banks of ferns and growth to Phil. "I'm not going to let him die, Rose. I promise."

"Dan...I don't know how to thank you. You saved his life. All our lives."

His blue eyes flashed and grew hard again. "Good for me."

"What do you mean?"

"If Grant had been flying, none of this would've happened. Because of my stubbornness, your regular pilot wasn't on the plane. A more experienced pilot—"

"Makes mistakes, too," Rose interrupted. "This isn't the first time Phil has flown the plane. And Grant's not always up there with him."

"I made sure of that, didn't I?"

"Oh, stop. I don't want to hear it. It's nobody's fault, including the poor geese."

After a long pause, Dan tilted his head and nodded. "Guess the birds really got the raw deal, didn't they?"

Relieved, Rose let her shoulders slump. "Yes, poor things. Least they can do is have landing lights if they're going to fly in our air space." All at once she shivered and glanced around. "Nobody's going to find us by dark, are they?"

"I doubt it."

"God, I hate the idea of sleeping out here. Can't we sleep in the plane?"

Dan shook his head. "There's a faint odor of fuel inside—I don't trust it. Better we stay out here. It's high and dry ground. After all, I promised to take you camping, remember?"

She managed a small smile, then shivered again. This time Dan slid his arm around her and drew her against him. His body was warm and receiving, his arm an anchor for her fears. She let her head drift onto his shoulder.

"Besides," he said gently, "the outdoors is a very welcoming place if you know how to read it."

"Read it?"

"Sure. It's warm, no dangerous wildlife around, the air smells better than 52nd Street, and right down there, around that knot of overgrowth, is a babbling stream of fresh water for you to take a bath in."

She tipped her head up. "How do you know? Did you go down there?"

"Rose, don't you watch adventure movies? There's always a babbling stream around the bend and down the hill for the beautiful leading lady to bathe in."

Rose laughed, feeling warm for the first time in hours. "Oh, sure. Complete with slime and water moccasins and alligators. Got any Calgon Bath Oil Beads? I can hardly wait."

"And I can't wait to see you." Provocative fingers caught a strand of her glowing red hair. "You know the script. I'll watch you in awe from the reeds. The sunlight will roll across your bare shoulders ...the moist ends of your hair will flick at me...I'll chuckle..."

Rose smiled. "Bet this is where the water moccasin comes in."

"Yes, and the script calls for the beauty to be rescued from the slimy water moccasin by the dashing leading man, who looks suspiciously like me. And, I must add, he does it with alarming panache. What do you say?"

"Well, I'd buy a ticket," she told him, "but I don't know if I'd play the lead."

"Oh, no?" Dan tipped her chin upward. "Let's have a screen test."

A faint taste of perspiration mingled with the scent of pine and other scents uniquely theirs. As their lips touched and moved against each other Rose submitted to his closeness. It was a journey into security, comfort, into the touch of a man unlike any other man she had known, into sensations that had been hinted at before but never truly fulfilled. No other man had succeeded in giving her all these components of love—the emotional closeness, the sense of coming home, the rush of happines, the dizzy physical flight brought by his touch. Why couldn't she trust him completely? Was there some flaw in her own character that held her back from the delirious high dive?

Now, out here, lost in the mountains with no points of reference or reality, it was easy to let go of the obligations and pressures of her life; too easy to forget commitments and responsibility. Lost in the moist trails of Dan's kisses, Rose became a nymph, heedless of any other existence. She felt her own limbs tingle, becoming the laurel tree of passion, the desire of a young god.

A wave of weakness made her head fall back as though in a faint, and his lips strayed to her throat and the soft curves of her shoulders, dipping into the recesses of her neck.

"Better now?" he whispered, cradling her in the long paling rays of the sun. The woodlands were streaked with buttery shafts of light, and the effect on her hair mystified him.

Rose nodded. "I was just thinking of my grandfather," she told him.

"Oh? That's not what I hoped you'd be thinking of."

Rose straightened her legs, and smoothed her skirt over her knees. "He was the only real relative I ever had. I didn't have a family like you did. Phil's parents treated me like a daughter, but Gran was my family. When he died... it wasn't real. And it happened so far away." She closed her eyes. Why was she thinking of this now, with the feel of Dan's lips still tingling on her throat?

"Athens, I heard," he said.

She looked at him critically. "How do you know that?"

"Well, it wasn't exactly a secret, Rose."

No, I guess not."

"And you can imagine that any headline saying 'Red MacKenzie' would catch my eye. After all, I used to work for him."

"Right. Sometimes I still expect him to come back." She blinked, and a tear broke from her eye onto her cheek. "Oh, no," she murmured, but too late. The tears kept coming. Her throat knotted, and suddenly Dan was drawing her against his chest, caressing her head and her shaking shoulders. "I feel..."

"I know," he whispered, sighing deeply as she pressed into his embrace.

"Stupid..."

Dan laughed sympathetically. "That's not quite what I expected you to say, but I know what you mean. Oh, Rose...don't regret so much. Things always look worse than they are."

He massaged her back and shoulders as though they were parts of his own body, as though he knew just how she wanted him to touch her.

She was crying now as the fear and the regret crushed in upon her and she found safety in his embrace, safety from the world she had conquered, safety within this green alien world with its one strong inhabitant—this man.

She sniffed back the tears and let herself think of her grandfather, of all the things that had ever meant anything to her, as though it could help her measure her feelings for Dan.

"When I was a little girl," she said slowly, settling against his chest, "about eleven, Gran took me back to Scotland. We hadn't been back since I was five, and I was smitten by the place. He knew I was at an age when my mind was a sponge, and he wanted to show me his old tramping grounds. We went straight to Glen Diath."

"Never heard of it," Dan said, prodding her to tell him more. In his mind he saw a needle-thin eleven-year-old, charmed by an ancient land, and he smiled.

"There's a castle there," she continued, "owned by an old R.A.F.

chum of Gran's. I'm sure it's still there. Sir John would never have sold it. God, at least I hope not. It was like a medieval gymnasium. Drafty, huge, hulking, but still very..."

"Mythological?" Dan supplied.

"Yes. Yes, exactly." Rose's eyes were fixed on the dusky sky behind the trees, but all she saw was the castle. "Sir John was a collector of statues. Statues everywhere."

"Sounds familiar," he said.

Rose nodded. "It had quite an effect on me. I just loved those statues, every last piece, but there was this one...a one-of-a-kind porcelain he had commissioned. It was about twelve inches high and it looked like it was made of silk. It was a statue of Flora MacDonald standing in a clutch of heather."

"Flora who?"

"A Jacobite patriot. She helped Prince Charles Edward Stuart escape from the British Army after the defeat at Culloden."

"Oh, good girl," he said smugly.

"Do you want to hear about my lurid past, or not?"

"Sure I do. Sorry."

His free arm folded across her breasts with warm intimacy, but there was something so basic and protective about the gesture that Rose didn't resist.

"The Flora statue was supposed to be a portrait of the moment that she watched the Prince's small boat go across the loch to Raasay, near Skye."

"Raasay near the sky? Sounds like a nice place."

"It is," she laughed. "Very nice." She slipped deeper into Dan's arms. "When I looked into her sweet porcelain face, I had to touch her. I reached out to run my finger down her tartain shawl—and Sir John nearly had a heart attack. Scared me to death, too. Dan, I only wanted to touch her. Nobody would ever love her more than I did at that moment, and I wouldn't have hurt her for my life, but—"

"But all he saw was a kid reaching for his costly little bauble. I can see it."

"Now I can, too. But then...I cried myself to sleep. He'd made me feel like I'd exposed myself in public. I'd lost my virginity to a work of art, and he wouldn't let me *touch*."

Exhausted by the effort of calling up old feelings, Rose's hand floated out toward the darkening evening. Dan's hand moved toward her fingers, and they laced together, gently.

"Sometimes," she whispered, "I still wake up at night, hungering to touch that porcelain shawl."

When he spoke, his voice in her ear was as potent as the memory of the wind across Lochalsh. His hand guided hers upward along his strong thigh. "I'll let you touch, Rose. And I'll do something no sculpture can do. I'll touch back."

And he wasn't teasing. The fullness beneath her hand proved that. He wanted her, she knew that. Yet, as erotic as the words were, the promise was gentle and soothing to her.

His other hand moved more firmly against her back. He turned her over into his lap, cradling her there.

She turned her whole body against his, transferring all the erotic need to touch that surged from her. Her eyes welled with tears when she saw the love in Dan's eyes and felt the heat pounding in his body.

He became her whole world, filling her mind and drowning out all the memory demons. Her senses dissolved under his touch as his fingers pressed deeply beneath her breast. A tingle rushed up from her toes. In a surge of arousal she pressed upward, her lips catching his. A glorious fatigue weakened her legs and all Rose could do was roll against Dan, pressing into his chest, hiding in his arms, lost.

The moment seemed unalterable. Never once did she feel as though she couldn't break the embrace if she really wanted to—the shackles holding her to him weren't these tender arms, this generous, wet, long kiss, but something else.

These bonds that held her now...it wasn't exactly recognition and nothing like experience, because Rose MacKenzie had never felt anything like this kind of benevolent need before. But she sensed her own womanhood rising up to recognize the bonds. Oh. Yes...she recognized them—as clearly as if they were flames burning against a black curtain.

They were the stinging shackles of a red-hot love.

"We shouldn't be doing this," Rose said. "Not with Phil lying there."

Dan shifted first against her, then away from her. She blinked, her lips suddenly chilled as the cool air came between the heat of their mouths.

Still holding her, Dan leaned back against the plane and cleared his throat. "I know," he said, and then nodded. His strong arm sat her upright and left her there as he stood up and walked away.

"Dan—" She struggled to her feet, still numb, wanting to chase the relationship that now was slipping away from her. But when had this turned into a relationship? At which moment, had his touch stopped being the touch of a stranger? When had it become a lover's touch? A thing of intimacy...

"Dan, please wait."

He paused in half-step, then turned around. His blue eyes were glazed with hurt.

"It's okay, Rose," he said. "It didn't feel right to me either. Maybe the time'll never be right for us."

No bitterness, no resentment. He might as well have been reciting a poem. Almost as though he realized how close he'd come to a goal that meant a great deal to him, only to have it slip away like an object in the fog.

Dan stepped through the ferns to where Phil lay on his makeshift bed of blankets and cushions. He knelt down beside Phil and looked at the pale face. He put his hand on Phil's chest to check the shallow breathing, then checked to be sure the shoulder wound had stopped bleeding.

"Dan, I'm sorry," she said, "but please don't get carried away in self—"

Dan's hand sliced toward her. "*Don't* say that. Just don't say that."

Rose started toward him, but he stood up and strode past Phil, making his escape into the wooded area beyond the plane's big body.

Rose stumbled over a fallen sapling, catching her ankle in the branches. "Dan, wait. I didn't mean—"

She stopped herself, reacting to a new instinct, one different from those instincts that had been confusing her over the last few minutes. She stopped short, right where she stood. She listened intently.

Birds...insects buzzing...leaves rustling...and...a regular sound, a thrumming noise, like traffic in the distance.

An engine.

Rose spun around, craning for a view through the trees above her.

"A plane! Dan! A plane!" she gasped, stumbling across the clearing, looking for an open spot in the green canopy. Within moments she was plummeting through the woods, out of sight of her own plane, following the buzz of a small plane engine above.

She dug her feet into a scrubby hill and climbed, branches scoring her arms and tearing at her clothing. The forest that minutes ago had been a charming haven once again became malevolent, trying to stop her from reaching high open ground. A bristly bush reached out and caught her sleeve.

"Let *go* of me!" she growled. She twisted toward the bush and actually slapped it, then plunged on.

She had to get to high, wide ground! A place to signal, to wave—

Like going up a set of stairs in the dark, her determined plunge upward made Rose stumble forward, her uphill foot jamming hard into the ground, and she fought to recover. The engine sound continued buzzing high in the sky, frustrating her as it faded in and out. Where was the damned clear ground?

"Ooooh...wait!" Rose thought she shrieked, but it came out a gasp.

Suddenly the boughs opened above her and she looked up at clear sky. It was a sky of fading light, the disturbing pinks and grays of sunset and nightfall.

Rose skidded to a halt. She squinted desperately at the wide sky, then at the uneven carpet of studded forest and rocky hills.

"Where are you?" she demanded, listening hard for the buzz of the engine. "Why don't you—"

A form plunged past her, and she jumped to one side. Branches snapped, leaves crackled as Dan came crashing through the bushes and grated to a stop just past Rose, scanning the sky.

"There they are!" he shouted, jamming a finger upward.

Rose moved around him until she could see where he was pointing, and indeed there was a shape in the sky, its wings fully profiled as it banked around for another sweep.

"Do they see us?"

"I don't know...they're too far north," Dan said, "but if that's not a search pattern, I'll eat my shoes!" He whirled and grasped Rose by the shoulders. "Our mayday got through! It got through!"

A squeal of joy flooded up from Rose and she started jumping up and down. Her hands coiled around Dan's arms and his around hers. Together they ran across the top of the hill toward the speck in the northeastern sky.

Suddenly Rose stopped short and stammered, "Shouldn't we...shouldn't we start a fire or something?"

"We could," he said, "but I doubt they'd see it. It's not dark enough for a fire, but not light enough for a column of smoke to make any difference. Damn! Who invented night anyway!"

Rose actually found a moment for a giddy laugh. "I was just wondering that about the trees."

"Well, so we think alike." Dan grabbed her hand again and pulled her farther out onto the hill. At once he pointed at the sky straight north and said, "There's another one!"

Once again Rose craned for a view, and sure enough, there was a second plane skirting the horizon.

"They're too far north," she said.

"That's where they expect us to be. They're crisscrossing. Probably the Civil Air Patrol." Dan glanced toward the sinking sun. "They'll have to stop soon—it'll be too dark to search. In the morning they'll probably widen their perimeter." He turned to her, the dusk giving his blue eyes a faint silvery cast, his bond hair a touch of the moon. He squeezed her arms gently. "All we have to do is batten down and weather the night."

The two planes, far distant behind Dan's shadowed form, wagged their wings to signal a break-off of the futile search and banked lazily toward the horizon. It was as though they heard Dan speaking. Rose watched them go, and felt her feet weighted to the ground.

The faint hum of engines faded, and winked out. Leaves once again rustled overhead in an evening breeze. Trees were a black serration against the horizon, outlined by the red setting sun. A cricket chirped, and it was suddenly night. Before her, Dan filled up her world.

Rose gazed at him through the paleness of dusk. "If it wasn't for Phil," she said quietly, "this would be almost like a dream."

He let go of her.

As he strode back into the woods, Dan paused a moment and glanced back.

"Lots of things would be dreams," he said, "if it wasn't for other things."

Rose lay alone beneath the sky that night.

The perfect silence called for abandon and release. The star-peppered sky, the blanket of crisp air...

If only he would come here and coil those strong arms around her again. Her dress wasn't enough for warmth tonight. Her breasts ached for another source. She sent a psychic invitation to him, but he resisted it and went on sleeping.

She raised her head and saw Dan lying in the thin moonlight, a cocoon with a blue-silver cap, all shades muted by night. She imagined running her hands under the blanket to find his thighs, imagined turning his lean hip until it settled into the contours of her own. He was making love to her even now, as they lay yards apart, calling, singing to her, begging, tasting, teasing.

Love him?

Rose raised herself on one elbow. She remembered bizarre minutes in her penthouse, the hypnotic confusion after he was gone, the haunting blue rose...the horror of the crash, thoughts of losing him, his generous concern for Phil...

She remembered thinking Dan too might be dead or hurt in that tangled cockpit. She couldn't pretend she didn't care anymore. Accidents were too chancy, too tragic. Like the one that had stolen her grandfather.

She had just rediscovered an old acquaintance in Dan, then nearly lost him.

Get over there or lose him for good. He walked out of our life once...he could do it again.

Rose pushed the blanket away and crawled to her knees. Cool air rushed over her bare thighs where the skirt had bunched up. To one side, she heard Phil's steady belabored breathing and knew he was lost in a healing sleep. It freed her.

Like a ghost she got to her feet, moved over the grassy ground, unreal as clouds against the black sky. Stars, moonlight, the forest trees provided a tapestry.

Dan lay on the ground before her. He was lying on his side, the blanket tucked up around his neck like a cowl. Rose tried to move closer, but she couldn't. He was too beautiful.

He groaned and rolled onto his back, bringing his face into a dusty shaft of moonlight. His features were ivory, his hair silver, with shadows of midnight blue and gunmetal gray. She caught a glimpse of eyelashes against his cheek. Where once there had been flesh and blood now was marble, a seemless beauty of sculpture. Would he shatter if she touched him?

Her hands quivered against her breasts as she tugged at the lips of her halter. Her eyes ached as she gazed down at Daniel in the moonlight. A threshold of intrigue slipped open. She had only to step though.

If she dropped her precious pebble into Daniel's pool how long before the ripples stopped spreading?

She trembled and crushed her fists against her prickling skin. Her face was hot.

She hurried back to her blankets, curled into them, pressed her hands between her thighs, and turned her hot face to the pillow.

Her body throbbed, but it throbbed alone.

Chapter Nine

MORNING CAME WITH bird songs, but unwelcome. Rose's night had been a blur of wishes, ragged hopes that Dan would sense her desire behind her cowardice. She had even hoped he would find his way to her blanket without her making a fool of herself by asking, but the hope had come alive only in restless dreams.

As Rose lifted her heavy head from the ground, she realized she was hearing more than the rustle of leaves. There was a scraping noise, wood against metal.

She sat up, blinked into the early morning light and focused on Dan's form, high up on top of the *Briar Rose.*

For several minutes, she watched him. He was dragging branches off the plane, shoving them down into the brush, clearing the long metal body so it could be more easily seen by search planes. His untucked shirt was partially unbuttoned, the sleeves rolled up to show forearms glistening with fine golden hairs, muscles flexing as he dragged the heavy broken branches away.

He wasn't going to let this situation beat him. She could see that in the way he yanked and hauled on those stubborn branches. He went out of his way to break the ones that wouldn't move. He would wrestle the defiant branches down and kick them until they cracked.

Rose could see the determination that the search planes wouldn't pass them by in his angry twisting body. Dan wasn't going to allow it.

The plane looked a lot bigger than it ever had before, and Dan was a long way up. How had he gotten up there?

She determined to get up there herself. As she moved in that direction, she got more perspective on Dan as he worked up above. His back was turned to her now, and she watched him as if in a trance. His rayon shirt pulled itself taut over the breadth of his shoulders, its tail flapping against tensed buttocks, every line of his strong legs showing through the tight jeans. But it was less the form of the man that attracted Rose than the pure substance of him.

Any man could have muscles, and any man could wear rayon shirts and snug jeans. Rare, though, was the man who moved like Dan was moving now, driving against the tide of fate and chance, his own determination his only real weapon.

And the sensation came again that she'd seen this—or a version of this—before. Now she knew where she had seen it: outside that tall window at the golf club.

Rose stood half awake, lost in erotic illusions. She was held by the vision of what might have happened last night, what she had wished for and failed to pursue. Her hands ached to play over those arms now hauling branches from the wreckage. But reality was Dan, high above and unaware of her, his body swaying against the force of the fallen trees.

On top of the plane, fighting for balance, Dan scraped about four layers of skin off his forearm, but he didn't care. He was coming out the winner against a branch as thick as his calf and that had enough leaves on it to hide half the fuselage. When those search planes came back, this hulk was going to be visible.

Because *he* couldn't be patient, Phil was lying there badly hurt. If there had been any delusions of chance in his mind, Dan couldn't see them anymore. Rose might turn to him in *this* wonderland, but she surely would look at him with different eyes once they hit the city. He knew his time was running out.

Dan took out his blunder after blunder on the branch. Leaves rattled all around him, like laughter.

With a great *crack*, the branch gave way and Dan forced it off the plane. Scraping all the way down, the branch seemed to take a whole forest with it. Leaves, vines, and webs slid down the curved surface of the fuselage and hit the ground with a loud, rustling thud.

He straightened up, wincing, but the stiff, harsh ache of his injured hip only added to his victory. At least he could best a chunk of wood.

He drew in a deep breath and regained his balance, then turned to see if there was anymore to be done.

And stopped.

There she was.

Standing there, on top of the plane. Her bare feet were planted firmly against the curved metal surface of the old war craft. Her white halter dress drew in the colors of the forest, her red hair mussed and glistening, outlined by the tall metal fin of the plane's tail. She might have been a wood nymph.

Dan straightened his back and shoulders. The aches he felt now dissolved in the green pools of Rose's eyes. Why was she here?

"Morning, firefly," he said calmly. "It's all done. You didn't have to come up."

He moved toward her. The woods separated them from the city, the plane separated them from the woods. They were as alone as they had ever been, here in the pale dawn light, on top of a massive slumbering beast.

Dan's chiseled arms glistened in the lemony dawn light, his hair a cap of bright wheat.

Rose suddenly found his gentle eyes very welcoming.

Barely above a whisper, he asked, "Why did you come up here?"

"I wanted to see you close up. In the light of day."

"And do you see *me?*" he asked. "Or that kid you used to know?"

"It's not fair," she said. "This isn't real. This place isn't real. You're not and I'm not. I don't want love through a haze. I want to know what I'm feeling and what the man I love is feeling."

"Sometimes it's our day-to-day lives that put things out of perspective. I want you alone, Rose. I want you to have me alone, away from the city, away from... him." He nodded downward. "Then I'll give you all the reality you can stand."

They stared into each other's eyes like a haunting echo and its caller.

They smelled each other and felt the closeness, the almost-touch, the almost-honesty.

"I don't know what you're afraid of," he added. "If I was going to rape you, I've had plenty of opportunity out here in the middle of nothing. If I was going to take advantage of you emotionally

. . . well, I'm beginning to believe that isn't possible with you, Rose." He cleared his throat. "Excuse me . . . I've got to get the flares out."

He slipped past her. Even though the plane was large, there wasn't much room on top, and their bodies brushed as he passed.

Although Rose stood facing the open woodlands, she saw in her mind's eye Dan as he stopped and prepared to slide off the top of the plane.

"I'll go with you."

She imagined him straightening again, turning to look at her with the same astonishment she felt herself. She felt his eyes as though they were fingers.

"Anywhere you want," she murmured. "One week. To get to know each other again . . . without the window between us."

His whisper was like a sonic boom on the horizon. "Are you playing games?"

"No," she told him. And this time she turned to face him, "I'll go."

He stepped closer—much closer—and cupped her face in his hands.

"I promise you," he said, "if you don't love me by the end of our time together, you'll never see me again."

Rose gazed at him. "Kind of a weird promise, coming from a smiling face."

Dan blushed then. "Am I smiling? Oops, I guess I am. Darn, there goes my tough-guy image."

"Let it go," she said, and she was smiling, too. "It's not that great. Besides, I have an ulterior motive."

"Which is?"

"Which is, if I go someplace with you, maybe I'll be able to find those skeletons you must have in your closet. Then I can shake the bones at you from time to time and keep you in line."

"You want skeletons?" he laughed. "How about the time I smuggled a truckload of Polynesian acrobats into the country and tried to open a circus?"

"Too comical," she said, starting to feel lightheaded. "I want sordid."

"My affair with Queen Bethula of Prussia?"

"No such person."

"Darn again. Thought I had you on that one."

"Sordid," she urged, realizing how absurd this was becoming. They were both escaping into silliness to avoid the discomfort of the deal she'd just accepted.

Dan rolled his eyes at the paling sky. "I'm a carrier of a rare tropical disease?"

Rose laughed. It felt good.

"Sordid! Not gruesome!"

"Mmmm," he mumbled, nodding. "Probably not the kind of thing to flag when you're trying to convince a sexy lady to marry you, is it?"

That made her nervous again, but she bullied it away. "Heck, if that's all you've got, you're a lot less interesting than I thought you were, Hedgeclipper."

Dan smiled self-consciously, and then the smile partially fell away as he caught the glint of greenery in the emerald of her eyes, and he moved closer still, until they were as close as possible without actually touching. They felt each other's breath, felt the warmth of the closeness pulsing between them, sensed the twitchy desire pulling at them and the mystery keeping them apart.

"You know," he said slowly, "if not for Phil, I don't think I'd be very anxious to be found. I could stand being marooned here with you."

Swallowing tensely, she responded, "Yes... it is beautiful here."

Dan's fingers found and encircled her wrists. "That's not what I mean. Without you here, it would be just another place."

His forefinger traced her jawline, her lips, then brushed beneath the red curtain of hair to find the pulsing artery in her throat.

As Rose melted against him, he murmured, "I could offer you all kinds of things but nothing you couldn't buy or sell with a snap of your fingers. All I really have is what you see before you."

His breath preceded the brush of his lips on hers, like an entreaty, gentle persuasion. His voice flowed like cream over strawberries.

"Let me be the one, Rose," he whispered. "I swear I'll never hurt you."

She was magnetized. Her lips parted in anticipation as his mouth fixed over them, and this time it was Rose who closed the space between their bodies, pressing herself aginst him in an answer that was as exciting as it was dangerous.

"Yes," she whispered. "Yes."

They were like children with a secret. They weren't sure if it was right or wrong, only that it was fun. Rose was glad Phil was lying over there, to provide a dose of common sense against her impulses, against her crazy wish to stay here in the woods. She was so close to the high dive...so near the edge...

It was Dan who slipped away before they had the chance to make love. Strange...it was supposed to be the woman who resisted.

He was baiting her, she knew. She'd promised to go away with him, and he was going to make sure that promise was preserved, rather than lose it in a brief sexual fling in the midst of near-tragedy. He was waiting for the right moment, the right place, and she darned well knew it. Because they *hadn't* made love, Rose felt like a schoolgirl who'd just been given a friendship ring by the cutest boy in class.

When the sun came up all the way, her head cleared. Kind of. She didn't regret anything exactly, not yet. She liked Dan. In spite of the aura that surrounded him like fog, she had started to recognize a little leap in her stomach when she caught a glimpse of him.

He was staying away from her right now, she knew that. She didn't blame him. He expected her to change her mind and tell him to forget the agreement to go away with him.

She wasn't going to break it.

A faint groan from under the plane's protective wing cut into her tangled thoughts. She shook herself back to the immediate situation.

She hurried to Phil's side. "Phil?"

He groaned again and blinked. "What is this? A hangover? God, it better have been a great party..."

"How do you feel?"

"Like what's left of the cheese dip..."

Rose brushed a flop of brown hair out of Phil's eyes and leaned over him. He was pallored, obviously weak, but he was alive, and it was morning. The search would start again soon.

"Oh, God...the plane. Oh, Rose, I'm an ass," Phil said. A boyish guilt surfaced in his brown eyes. "I should've known better than to come out of the clouds so low. I could've killed us all..."

Rose smiled, glad to see the sparkle returning to his eyes. "Go ahead and feel guilty, I don't care. As long as you're okay, I really don't care."

"Where's Dan?" he asked. "Is he all right?"

"He's looking for the flares."

"They're in the aft compartment on the port side, tell him."

"He'll find them," she said evasively.

Phil blinked up at her and tried to focus on her pretty face. "He's a handy guy to have around."

Rose leered at him. "Is that a nudge or a fishing line?"

He shrugged his good shoulder, and even that simple gesture took all the strength he had, leaving him pale and breathless.

"Little of both, I guess," he muttered. "How about you? Are you okay?"

With a sigh she answered, "Oh, sure..."

Phil craned his neck to get a look at the plane, its belly buried in overgrowth. "Poor old *Briar Rose*. She made it through the war and forty years of Red's roughhousing, and all it took was me and a few stupid birds to bring her down. I'm glad Red's not here to see this. He'd probably turn me over his knee like he used to. He always said I'd never get so big he couldn't take me out behind the stable and reinstill the authority."

"She'll fly again," Rose promised him. "I'll salvage her. I don't care what it costs."

Phil nodded dubiously. "Funny how you get used to having some people around, isn't it?"

Rose was surprised by her own reaction to Phil's words. Her thoughts weren't with her grandfather, but rather inside the plane with Dan.

She shook herself. "We saw planes last night. We think they were searching for us."

"That means the mayday got out."

"Yes, that's what Dan said."

Phil blinked some of the glaze from his eyes and asked, "Did Dan say anything else I should know about?"

"Like what?"

"Like anything."

"Oh...Phil. You're not going to believe it."

"What?"

"He told me who he is. He's the boy greenskeeper who used to work around the Coachman Long Island back when we were about fourteen. He used to stare at us through the restaurant windows.

"I don't believe it." Phil shook his head and stared at the trees.

"Danny the Hedgeclipper! I *hated* that kid!"

"I know you did," Rose laughed.

Rose tried to glance away before a telltale flicker showed up in her eyes, but she knew she'd failed. Phil had seen the flashing ambivalence, the complications that had arisen since they had taken off from the airport. No matter how she tried to hide it, no matter how the early morning shadows still played on her face, she knew Phil could tell.

"Rose," he began cautiously, "what's going on?"

Rose licked dry, unglossed lips, felt the fullness of her own mouth and remembered the taste of Dan's.

"Now that I know who he is..."

"Oh, no..."

"I told him," she admitted, "I'd go away with him for a while."

Phil's expression stiffened. It was several seconds before he could bring himself to push a phrase out.

"He doesn't waste a minute, does he?"

Suddenly it was Rose's turn to feel guilty, guilty that she and Dan had found passion during Phil's pain.

Not bothering to regain control over his expression, Phil asked, "Where?"

"Doesn't really matter where."

"What does matter?"

If only she had an answer to that! Wouldn't it be nice to know? Wouldn't it be nice to sweep these feelings under the rug and walk away over them, just as she had always done to her problems?

Maybe she could have Dan freeze-dried and added to her sculpture collection. Then he could be around, and she would stay in control.

"Rose," Phil began with effort, "that's not all there is."

"What do you mean?" she asked. "Of course that's all there is. He's that kid. Now that I know, I recognize him perfectly. Why would there be anything else?"

"I don't know. But maybe men sense something about other men that women just don't key in on. I'm telling you there's more to him. Know what else?"

"What?"

"I get the feeling that even *he* doesn't like the rest of his own story, and that's why he's not telling it."

Rose rubbed Phil's good arm and said, "Honey, you've been

unconscious. You haven't been with him. You haven't seen him working to save all our lives...especially yours."

"I know, I know. I'm not saying he's a bad person. I just—I don't know. There's more. There's got to be more. I just can't believe he's gone through all this rigamarole just to turn out to be the gardener from fifteen years ago."

"Why are you really so suspicious of him, Phil?" she asked introspectively. "What's he really done that makes both of us so afraid?"

They were silent for a moment.

"Rose, I have a confession," Phil said then. "I like him."

That made her look down in question.

"I like him," Phil repeated, "and that scares the hell out of me. Likeable people don't go around hiding their pasts. They don't have to. They don't get lost in corporate shuffles either. How come his name is known, but only vaguely? There's got to be more to him. I'd be a lot more comfortable if you'd postpone your 'going away' until I can do some more snooping."

Rose licked her lips contemplatively, to see if she liked the taste of this conversation.

"Decisions like this can't be made with a calculator, Phil," she said softly. "They have to be decided by the heart..."

She stopped herself. Was this Rose MacKenzie talking?

Phil was looking at her very dubiously now.

"Rose," he began, "every time you push against yourself, you sound less and less convinced."

"I'd be lying if I said he didn't make me think," she said.

Phil's lips curled in a mxiture of reactions. "I'm afraid to ask what he makes you think of. I don't know if it's smart to hand that much rope to a man like Dan."

"Maybe not, but..."

"But? There's a 'but'?"

She nodded. "Phil...I think I'm falling in—"

"Oh, no!" he blurted. "Please don't say it."

She gazed at him tenderly and said, "It's so hard to think sometimes."

She ripped out a handful of grass and tossed it at him.

He raised a hand to ward off the playful rain, and instantly his energy drained away. "Oh, boy..." he moaned.

Rose rubbed his arm sympathetically. "Still weak?"

"Guess so."

"I'll get something for you to eat. You need strength."

She started to get up, but he caught her hand and held tight.

"Rose, listen to me," he entreated, indulging in a touch of emotional panic. God, what she'd almost said! Did she mean it? "You've got to decide what you want. I can't take action unless I know what you want. Do you want me to keep looking? If he's got a dark side," he added slowly, "do you still want to know?"

She didn't answer soon enough; she simply didn't have the answer ready.

At least not before Dan appeared over them.

"Well, what's this? Meeting of the board?"

He knelt on the other side of Phil and both Phil and Rose suddenly felt guilty that they'd been talking about him as though he was some kind of pirate who'd planned all this. But then maybe he was.

"Morning," he said to Phil. "You feeling any better?"

"Better than unconscious, yes," Phil told him.

"That's good. You had us both shook up." Dan reached over to the dressing on Phil's injured shoulder. "Let me check this. Probably needs a fresh one."

"I'll do it," Rose said eagerly. At last a chance to help. "I'll get everything and heat some water and be back in a minute."

The two men watched her leave. There was an art to watching Rose MacKenzie, her hair the color of dark exotic rubies, her green eyes flashing beneath straight brows. The cream dress cupped her breasts, the jersey skirt swirling around her long legs—each man was left wanting as she disappeared inside the grounded DC-3. She was elegant, even ornamental, breathtaking. Yet it wasn't necessarily her beauty, her height, or her poise that made her so attractive. She had a loveliness in her soul that few wealthy young women ever developed, and to the two men that transitory beauty of manner and humility was far more valuable than either would admit.

Phil cleared his throat and deliberately kept himself from mentioning Rose. It wasn't easy. There was always a "wow" waiting on his breath when she took off in one of those flourishes. How had that stringbean girl grown up into such a stunner?

Forcing himself back to reality, he asked, "Dan, did I see you limping?"

Dan blinked, tore his eyes away from the door of the plane, and looked at Phil.

"What? Oh...yeah, a little. I've counted thirty-two bruises so far. I'm going for the record."

"God, I'm really sorry," Phil said. "I thought I was the only one who was hurt."

Dan shook his head and shrugged. "There's a lot around here for both of us to be sorry about, isn't there?"

"Is there?" Phil countered. "You just ate the canary and I know it. Rose told me."

"Told you what?"

"That she's agreed to go off with you someplace."

"I see," Dan said, eyebrows lifting with a sudden candor. "And you think it's a mistake?"

"Yes. Sorry, but I do. Where are you going to take her?"

"That's our business. She's an adult, Phil," Dan said evenly. "You've got to stop protecting her."

"Nope," Phil said. "I won't ever. I told you that before."

"So I should consider this fair warning, right?"

"You can if you want to. Warnings don't seem to have much effect on you, Dan. All I can do is..." His voice faded and he let his head drop back.

"Phil?" Dan leaned over him. "Are you okay?"

"I'm okay."

"You turned pale all of a sudden," Dan told him, looking at him with annoyingly selfless concern.

"No, I'm okay, really."

Dan settled back, frustrated by the situation. "We'll get you to a hospital as soon as we can. I wish there was more I could do. I've been to the highest ground I could find, but I couldn't see any signs of civilization."

"It's not your fault," Phil said weakly. "Besides, I'm not very patient with being a patient. Rose'll tell you I'm notorious for checking myself out of hospitals."

"Sounds like my father."

"Intelligent man." Phil absently rubbed his left arm.

"Don't touch it," Dan said, moving Phil's hand away. "Don't want it to start bleeding again."

"No...old wounds bleed sometimes. Dan, Rose told me who you are. Danny the— " Dan chuckled and threw both hands up between them. "Please! Don't say that name. Bad enough she remembered it, never mind you. I always hated that name."

Phil looked at him candidly. "I always hated *you*."

With an honest little shrug, Dan said, "I know you did. It's not so different now, is it?"

"I don't hate you now—that's not what I meant."

"I know. But both of us here, with Rose...again. Years go by, but things don't change that much sometimes."

"Dan?"

"Hm?"

"I didn't give her the rosebud," Phil confessed. "It's still in my briefcase."

"You didn't give her—oh...that. In all the spin, I forgot all about it. I wasn't thinking clearly when I asked you to do that."

"Well, I don't know if Rose is thinking clearly or not," Phil said slowly, "and I wouldn't want this to sound like a warning, but— "

"But that's what it is, right?" Dan raised his brows.

Phil met the blond-blue-eyed looks that surely Rose was attracted to, and this time he mustered up all the strength it took to sound forceful as he spoke.

"Yes. That's what it is. You can go away with Rose. But I want you to know, and remember, while you're there, that every minute you're enjoying yourself and trying to get Rose to enjoy you, I'm going to be searching. If there's something more about you that you're not telling her, I'll be ready to do the telling by the time you get back."

"Fair enough. You make it sound as though I'm secretly a vampire or something."

"It's the 'or something' that worries me," Phil said.

"All I want," Dan told him, "is to get Rose far enough away that the Coachman trivialities aren't distracting her."

Phil allowed himself a knowing smile. "A multi-million-dollar string of restaurants and clubs doesn't have trivialities. It has painful details. Besides, I think the moon is all booked up this season."

"Is that your subtle way of saying it won't work?" Dan asked, "Or is it your way of keeping me from taking her away from you?"

Phil gazed at him in amazement. "Damn. You really are a smug son of a bitch in a lot of ways, aren't you?"

Dan nodded. "Maybe. Don't you think Rose deserves a chance at happiness?"

Phil let his eyes fall out of focus for a long, introspective moment. He reviewed his life at Rose's side, always an arm's length away. His legs knotted with private hunger as he lay there on the ground.

"I want happiness for her more than I want it for myself," he said solemnly, astonished at his own honesty at this minute. Then his eyes cleared suddenly and he looked at Dan. "You've had your way at every turn, and things still haven't gone the way you want with Rose. I'm not sure taking her away will change anything."

Sunlight broke through a thready cloud, making yellow streaks in the pre-dawn forest, and a bird who had been singing in a nearby tree chose this moment to fly away.

Silence fell around the two men.

"You take her away with you," Phil said. "But she'll be coming back to me. And don't forget...every minute you have her alone, I'll be here, looking for your past."

Dan raised his chin slightly, a gesture that could've been interpreted a dozen ways, and he was deliberately vague.

"I won't forget. But here's something for you to keep in mind. You're a decent guy, Phil, and I don't want to fight you. But I'm going to make Rose love me. I don't care the cost or the time it takes. I've spent half my life wanting it, and it'll finally be all or nothing."

His face hardened and when he spoke his tone was stained with conviction.

"I want it all."

Chapter Ten

SHE CHOSE SCOTLAND. It was to those dusky, snarled mountains, the cities and towns nestled between them, that she went with this man who said he loved her. She pretended the locale didn't matter, but it did. She wanted to see how the man measured up against the tapestry of her ancestral territory. Gran had always said things like that. "To check a worth, measure it against something you're sure of."

And within Scotland, there was Glasgow. A city with a smokestack and dockyard reputation, Glasgow turned out to be rather a surprise. Hardly the stuffy place Gran had always called the "arse of the Empire," this was a city whose buildings reached back into the 1400s, whose carved masonry and friendly manner put to rest all the dull things ever said about it. It was also a city undergoing a rigorous facelift. There was scaffolding everywhere—buildings being built, rebuilt, renovated, sandblasted. When Rose and Dan paused near their hotel to simply look at an ornate doorway, at least three people paused along with them, and two of them bothered to explain the building's history. One of them jovially repeated an old Glaswegian joke—that Glasgow would be very nice when it was finished.

The friendliness was contagious, and in its way it was dangerous.

Dangerous because it made Rose feel far too good about this whole arrangement. She *did* feel good. She felt happy. The commitment to a week's vacation made her happy; the plane ride—with its buffer of hours between New York and Prestwick—made her happy. The idea of getting the question solved in a few days made her happy.

Dan made her happy. During the whole trip he had been nothing but attentive and kind to her, nothing but a gentleman. His language had been impeccable—but it always had. Until the plane crash, her opinion of him had been one of bruskness and brashness, and yet she couldn't remember a single time he had made a rude remark or implied something she didn't *really* want him to imply. Now, though, with her right where he wanted her, Dan still acted completely at ease, didn't gloat over her decision in his favor. In a way, she wished he would. Then perhaps the coming decision wouldn't keep getting harder.

Dan Masters had grown from the sweaty, nervous boy into a man who wouldn't put up with a vague relationship—he'd made that clear. He meant not just to sleep with her or have an affair, but to marry her. The legalities of that were frightening to a woman of Rose's wealth, yes, but so was the emotional commitment. Dan understood power, certainly, and he understood possession.

Funny, but right now Rose didn't feel possessed...and that was exactly the way she'd expected to feel during this one-week promise, this short-termed commitment he'd maneuvered her into making.

Had he maneuvered her? She couldn't tell, couldn't see clearly through the haze anymore.

The haze Dan Masters spun around her like a master weaver. He did it with a touch on her arm, a guiding hand on her waist, the princely manner with which he took care of her in the city, the elegant way he treated her, the easy sense of humor, the witty remarks that kept her smiling, the courteous brush of his lips against her cheek, the reserved passion of his lips on her own when he kissed her in a different way—in fact, she'd never felt so well cared for. And that wasn't what she'd expected.

Hadn't Phil implied that she'd be too vulnerable if she agreed to this? Where was the vulnerable feeling? Hadn't she expected to feel possessed, put upon, and pressured? It just wasn't happening that way. This adventure seemed like many things—exciting, questionable, unpredictable—but above all it seemed to be the one thing Rose couldn't have predicted. It seemed *right*.

And the blue roses...they were everywhere. She was in a fairyland of blue blooms. Three dozen full blooms, with delicate serrated leaves, in a single elegant silver vase greeted her when the porter opened the door to the hotel suite. And again at dinner Dan somehow had arranged for blue buds to adorn their table. He must have been planning and arranging since the moment they'd been rescued.

That awful, confusing segment was over, yes. Phil hadn't spent more than two days in the hospital, but Rose had refused to leave New York until he was well enough to move around. Strangely, Phil himself had encouraged her to get going, mostly because he wanted her to get this week out of her system, she thought, and probably out of Dan's, too. She had thought he might take advantage of his condition to get her to stick around, but he hadn't.

She'd get old and gray and musty before she forgot the vision of Phil standing there in his bathrobe, his left arm in a sling, his brown hair ruffled, bidding her to stop fussing, get out, get it over with and come back safe. Safe... as though Dan Masters was actually dangerous.

Maybe he was.

Phil Van Dyke lay on his sofa bed, his injured shoulder aching in the sling. His good shoulder ached from hunching up against the telephone all morning.

"McCall? Yes, it's me. I'm fine, just fine. Listen, I want you to—what? No, of course not. I don't care what the newspapers said. It was just an accident. We came out of the clouds into a flock of birds. Mac, pay attention. This is gonna stink."

Phil took a deep breath and shifted his stiff neck. He caught a glimpse at the big clock on the wall. Rose had been in Glasgow, with Dan, for about five hours.

"Mac, I want you to pull out all the stops. We got a little information on him, and I want you to see if you can track it backward, then forward again and get something more out of it. Quit being polite and careful. Go after rumors. Talk to secretaries, clerks, waiters, anybody you can think of, and get all the gossip. Nothing is too implausible to report. Stop waiting for hard detail and go after the soft information. Maybe we can add it up into something concrete. Yes... I'll authorize anything you have to do. That's right.

I'm done playing softball—what? Hang the cost, Mac. Yes, really. Rose's future is at stake here. You ready? Okay, here's what we know..."

They were sharing a suite. Rose had expected that. The time had come, she knew that. Big girls could handle it.

She was determined to be a big girl.

But then Dan touched her hand and stood up from the dinner table, leaving the blue roses in their bud vases, and asking her with his silent eyes to join him in their suite.

Rose stood up. She took his hand. The magic went with them.

But none of her expectations prepared her for the changes in their suite between when they had checked in and when they returned after dinner. The rooms were now resplendent with the slight-of-hand that was Daniel's own way.

There were blue satin sheets on the bed and a shimmering periwinkle duvet on the floor now. Candles were shining everywhere, in silver candleholders, surrounded by arrangements of the notorious blue rose. On the plush pink carpet there was a trail of blue rose petals and buds as wide as a man's stride. The trail, veined with twisting satin ribbons, led through the main room and right to the bed. Here and there among the blue were roses of cream and peach colors. They lay with the blue roses on the vanity, tumbled among the duvet's satin folds on the carpet, on the silver tray where their soft scent mingled with the steaming aroma of tea from beneath a lace cozy. There were large blue blooms floating in scented fingerbowls beside the tea tray, a cake adorned with blue frosting buds and dark green serrated frosting leaves.

Rose murmured his name softly without looking at him, hypnotized by the wonderland, and heard a faint click as he shut the door behind her. The world was closed out.

Dan took her hand once again, very much the prince of this story, and drew her into the candlelit world of roses. There was music playing.

Until now, she hadn't really noticed the music. She'd heard it vaguely when Dan opened the door before her, but now it was part of the loveliness, as though things would be wrong without it. Especially when Dan came around in front of her, cupped her waist, and drew her into a soft and simple waltz. He knew what she needed. Reassurance that she wasn't being taken advantage of, a sense of belonging, a sense of his desire for her and no woman other than her.

He danced her into the fantasy, and she was willing to go. His body against her was solid but soft, his face up close, his touch as welcome as morning, his passions as real and readable as her own. He was warm to the touch as Rose slowly undressed him, gentle as he returned the gesture. Their clothing slipped unnoticed to the rose petals.

They shared everything, every touch, every moist kiss, caresses going back and forth like a tide between them. No matter how Rose tried to think straight—and she wasn't really trying that hard—there was too much Dan swirling through her body. His kisses filled her mouth, his loins hardened in seige at the base of her being, and they slipped together onto the satin duvet on the floor. They laughed as they realized they'd missed the bed altogether.

Rose let her smile carry her away as she gazed at his smiling mouth, then cast herself forward and gathered that mouth to her own. She lolled against him in lazy surrender, working her magic on him and begging him to reciprocate. He drew on the well of sensual music they made together. She gave in to herself, volunteering her body to the soaring storm that yanked her off the edge and plunged her into a sea of sensation.

He was tremendous, matching the fiery tumult of Rose MacKenzie with his own passion. Rose could have married any of a hundred anxious men, but none would have been able to surpass the wildness, the tenderness, the harmonic flight of delirium she reached with Dan. She was glad to be lost in love for him, and she was glad to say she loved him. It made a difference as she murmured those words against the soft skin beneath Dan's ear, a difference that he heard the words and let Rose feel the joy they brought him.

Through the crazy, errant lovemaking, a dozen rose petals left the floor and clung to their sweat-glazed skin. How surprising the rightness of his hand moving along her inner thigh. How arousing to feel the tiny tear-shaped petals clinging to the glaze of their desires for each other, testimonials to something Rose would never have predicted for herself even a month ago. How different the future suddenly appeared—and how exhilarating!

Dan made love to Rose as though it was the last time, not the first. He poured every sensuous, insane bit of ardor into the process of arousing her and himself. His fingers moved on her legs, her lips, her back, her shoulders. Rhythm after counterrhythm consumed them, working against needs, filling the void within Rose, heating the desire in Dan to experience the wholeness of this one woman. Together they twisted, surged, spun, tumbled, hand to leg, mouth on mouth, and they laughed and had fun.

Rose was lost in sensation. So lost that at times she forgot to consider Dan, pulling and clawing at him. She was utterly, deliriously, finally happy.

Happy...happy with Dan Masters. Happy, and in love.

And she thought she knew exactly what tomorrow would be like.

Chapter Eleven

"MISS MACKENZIE?"

"Yes?"

"I have your New York call through now."

"Thank you. Put him on."

The line went dead for a moment, then clicked and there was suddenly substance on the other end.

"Rose?"

"Hi, I'm here. How are you?"

"I died and you didn't even send one of those blue roses he keeps giving you."

"Poor you. Don't you feel good?"

"You've been gone two whole days. How should I feel? Have you been...enjoying yourself?"

"I almost hate to admit it," she said, lowering her voice, "but I've been having the best time of my life. I never thought I'd enjoy Glasgow so much, but I love it."

"Oh? What else have you been enjoying?"

Rose was silent for a moment. She glanced at the closed bathroom door and listened thoughtfully to the sound of the shower. She'd almost gone in there with him. Last night they'd taken a warm blue bath together. Blue, scented water with rose petals and daisies floating in it. What a sense of romance! Most women wouldn't even think of such things, much less a man.

"Phil," she murmured, "I think I love him. Does that sound ridiculous?"

After a moment, the overseas line actually sighed.

"Maybe as ridiculous as trying to paddle against a tidal wave," he said slowly. "I hope it's what you want for yourself, Rose."

A chill ran through her.

"If you're happy," he said, "if you love him... then I'm happy, too."

"Oh, Phil, thank you," she said softly.

"What the hell. Maybe he plays pool."

"You can always teach him," she said, laughing. "Taught me, didn't you?"

"Yes, may I never forgive myself. Rose, I want to believe him as much as you do. I like him, I told you that. We had to work pretty closely together in that cockpit—hell, the guy saved my life. But even the best passions can go sour. And you don't know much about him. He could be pretending to be something he's not. Actors do it every day. Don't buckle before you're sure. That's all I'm asking."

Rose listened, listened hard. She also listened to her own heart, to see if the nagging little doubts and fears were still there. But there was nothing—those doubts had been replaced by something else.

"Part of loving somebody," she said, "is having confidence in him."

Phil was quiet for a moment. "So..."

"So keep looking. I think Dan's past will stand up for itself."

"I sure as hell hope so. I'll call you if I get anything, and you can tell me then if you want me to keep on going. I'm going to ask you every time we talk, Rose."

The shower stopped, and almost immediately Dan strode out, wrapped in two towels, his body glistening, his hair wringing wet. Rose looked at him and smiled.

"If I'm in all the way," she said to Phil, "I want to know what I'm in."

There was a pause on the other end.

"He just walked in, didn't he?" Phil deduced.

Dan ran a towel over his hair and asked, "Is that Phil?"

Rose nodded. "That's right," she said to both men at once.

"Let me talk to him."

At this, Rose covered the mouthpiece and asked, "You want to talk to him?"

"Sure." Dan strode over to her. "Let's have it."

He held his hand out for the receiver, giving the impression that he'd stand there, dripping, all day if necessary.

Was it a power play? Reminding Phil that Dan was here and he wasn't?

Rose hesitated. She didn't want Phil's feelings any more hurt than they'd already been.

Finally Dan simply took the receiver from her and flipped it up to his ear.

"Phil? How's the shoulder?...Sure, I feel respons—well, I do, anyway. Good. That's a relief." He paused, listened, looked at Rose, and grinned. "Yes. Yes, we are...You bet she is. I think it's good for all of us. I'm looking after her. By the way, if you can't reach us for a few days, you won't panic, right?...I don't know. We might leave the city or get kidnapped by a tribe of Celts or something spontaneous like that." Another glance at Rose as he signed off made her uncomfortable. "I'm glad you're okay. I'll sleep better... what?" He glanced one more time at Rose, and this time his eyes clung to hers. "No, I'm not forgetting. Right...take it easy, now. Bye."

He hung up without giving her the chance to say goodbye to Phil.

"What are you not forgetting?" Rose asked.

"That's between Phil and me," he said cagily.

"Oh, fine. What next? You beat your chests and bellow at each other?"

Dan smiled, finger-drying his blond hair. "Me and Phil? I doubt it. We'd get drool on our Guccis." He wrapped the towel tighter around his thick firm waistline and ran the other towel up and down his arms. "Phil and I are the Laurel and Hardy of the MacKenzie frontier," he said. "We're like gentleman boxers. 'Do you understand that I'm going to hit you now? Are the rules clear to you?' 'Yes, I understand. Of course, I may hit back, you know.' 'Yes, I would expect that. I'm going to begin now. Are you prepared? You won't be surprised?' 'No, no, I won't be surprised. Of course, I intend to brace myself. I wouldn't want you to hurt your hand.'"

Rose laughed, even though she tried not to. It really was an accurate picture, and her heart warmed toward both of these men. The fact that they actually liked each other in spite of the competition gave an adult edge to the friction, and in many ways was quite a compliment to Rose. The fact that such men would be attracted to her...how much more could a woman ask for?

"It's all kind of comical," Dan said, "except that there's this dilly of a trophy."

Rose stood up from the vanity and tightened the green silk robe around her body. "I wish you wouldn't talk about me like that."

"Like what?"

"Like the deciding factor will be a friendly game of darts or something."

"Mmmm...good point. My mistake."

"You know, Dan," she said as she stepped up to the lace-covered table and poured herself a cup of the freshly delivered tea, "I can't figure you out."

He gave her a wicked little smile and said, "You figured me out pretty good last night, my dear."

She waved her hand at him. "Doesn't Phil present any threat to you at all? Is he really such a joke to you?"

The smile fell away. "Why do you ask?"

"Because he's no joke to me," Rose said firmly. "I won't let him be the brunt of yours."

"Who says I want to make him the brunt of anything?" Dan said, suddenly serious. "Did I ever say I wanted to hurt Phil? Or anybody? You know, you've made it all up that I've got some mysterious master plan you haven't discovered yet. Have you two always been like this?"

"Like what?"

"Presenting a united front, assuming the assault is coming."

Rose meandered toward him and plucked at the folds of the towel at his waist. "Getting defensive again, are we?"

His rosy cheeks puckered as he tried not to smile. "Caught," he said.

"Poor baby."

"Oh, pleeeeze...I really hate being cooed at."

"Ooooh..."

He balked as she backed him up against the vanity. After a moment, he tilted his head and put his finger on the moist circle of her lips.

"Well...your mouth is kind of cute, all oval like that, I guess ..." He grunted as she pressed against him and leaned her little oval into the soft lines of his own lips. "Mmmm...this is a test..." he muttered. "For the next thirty seconds, you will be lost in temptation..." He gathered her against him.

Rose let out a little groan and murmured, "Well, Clark Gable you're not, but I guess you'll do for now."

Not Clark Gable? I can fix that."

He pulled away and disappeared into the bathroom. Rose heard a faint rustle, then silence. When Dan reappeared, he had a skinny black lounge-lizard moustache drawn onto his lip.

"What is *that?*" Rose squealed and burst out laughing.

"It's pure masculinity," he said, striding toward her, shoulders back, eyes narrowed, and chest out. "It's raw manhood. Unculled sexual power. It's—"

"A bird! It's a plane! It's—"

"It's *eyeliner!*"

He struck an appropriate pose, muscles flexed, then whipped the towel from around his neck, flapped it once around, and donned it like a cape.

Rose almost fell over.

By the time he loosened his pose, she was actually gasping.

"What?" he wondered. "It's not erotic?"

Rose started to say, "Maybe it's aerobic," but all she got out was "Mayb—mayb—" before she had to bend over just to get a breath amid the sobs of laughter.

Dan's face took on an injured expression and he looked down at himself, attired only in towels and a drawn moustache. "This is what you get." he muttered. "Try to be macho, try to be Gable, and you get Barnum and Bailey. Woman, you are unappreciative."

He folded his arms and looked indignantly at the ceiling.

Rose clamped her mouth shut, wrapped her arms around herself, and started shaking. After a minute the laughter squeezed out of her.

Dan screwed his mouth up into a knot and scowled at her. "Nerve! C'mere, dame."

He swaggered over to her in swashbuckling style, which was rather ruined by the towel effect, swept her up into the crook of his right arm, and mashed his mouth against hers to smother the laughter. When he jerked his head back, the characterization broke—and it was his turn to laugh.

"Oh, perfect!"

Rose turned enough to see their reflection in the vanity mirror, and there on her face was an impression of his moustache.

"Don't say I never give you anything," he advised.

She laughed again. "I don't think Vivien Leigh had this problem."

"Vivien Leigh," he said, "didn't have *me*."

"That's it!" She snatched a felt-tipped pen off the side table and came at him. "I'm going to draw on you."

"Rose! Now wait a minute! Rose!" He grabbed her wrists and they both went over. Being on top, she had the advantage, but he had the muscle. Even so, it was a lot harder to hold her off than he would have admitted to his friends.

"How about an anchor that says 'Mary Lou'?" Rose threatened, bracing her foot against the bed for leverage. "Or a butterfly on your cheek? Don't you think you'd look darling with a butterfly on your cheek?"

"Rose, that's permanent ink!" He dug into the carpet as the tip of the pen brushed his nostril.

"You knew I was headstrong," she said, unremitting.

"I can sue you for disfigurement! No court in the land would blame me if I walked in with a butterfly on my cheek!"

He took a deep breath and vaulted upward, spinning in mid-air and reversing their positions, pinning her beneath him and pressing her wrists to the carpet. "I have you now."

"The heck you do," she panted. "I can still bite."

"Promise?"

The fire between them worked its magic on him as he gazed down at her, his eyes a holocaust. She was as precocious as a young cat. She looked up at him without blinking, and laughed.

"You drew on me first," she said, wrinkling her nose over the smeared eyeliner. "Now I have to fly to Paris for a facial."

"Frankly, my dear, I don't give a damp." He shook his wet hair over her like a setter just emerging from a lake.

"Dan! Yuck! I'm clean!"

"No problem. My thoughts are dirty enough for both of us."

His mouth clamped down on hers again, and this time the laughing faded away beneath the sensual pressure. Her body moved against his, her arms coiling around the fullness of his bare back, urged on by the movement of his hands on her.

Rose's eyes filled with tears in reaction as Dan slid his lips down her body to between the lapels of her green silk robe, moistening the skin beneath her breast. A moment later she was lost in the tingling backwash.

"Dan..." she whispered.

His breath was hot against her skin. "Rose, I feel like there isn't enough time for everything I want with you."

"I promised you a week," she said, surfacing from his caresses with effort. "Only two days are gone. After that...who can say? Who could've said I'd have felt the way I did when the plane was crashing and I thought I might lose you both?"

"I thought you'd have welcomed the chance to get rid of me."

"I thought so, too. But I was wrong. It hadn't hit me until then how much of a dent you'd made in my life—so quickly."

"A good dent or a bad dent?" he asked, gazing at her.

Rose pressed her lips into a thoughtful line. "When Gran died, I found out how much love can hurt. Sometimes it seems like too big a risk, and I get nervous about the feelings I'm having for you. It would be much safer not to love at all."

He drew her even closer against him. "How could that be? No love at all? Love is an investment, Rose."

Rose looked down, avoiding his eyes, afraid she might see too much of herself in them. What was he thinking of her right now?

As close as she felt to him, she did realize—as Phil had pointed out—that they knew each other very little. They were like flowers in the same garden—close and alike, yet still separated by a patch of mysterious soil. Intriguing, but mysterious and still dark. She began to wonder if she wasn't giving away too much of herself without demanding the same from him, but it seemed so easy now to give herself to Dan.

All thought now fled at his touch, his very nearness, the sensation and scent of him. All was charged with a light that brightened the dim corners of Rose's wants, bringing into sharp definition that which had been dull until now. She felt her body absorbing him with every breath, priming to receive him. Her body was throbbing. If he didn't make a move soon, she knew she would make it for him.

But he did. The towel around his waist fell away.

His voiced threaded into her mind and tugged at it as his lips played along her neck. "I know that something inside keeps telling you there's more to life than money," he whispered, "even lots of money. Maybe that's why I love you."

The embrace tightened, their movements quickening, and the bell-tone resonance of their bodies calling to one another became deafening. Suddenly they were being washed back to sea.

When he spoke, it was wind over water. "Rose, I want you again...I want you again."

Her single, poignant response was to let the robe slip off her shoulders and cup her back like a shawl, baring to him all the open ground of herself and her soul.

She pushed her hips against him, lost in her own surging motion, and huskily whispered, "Aren't you lucky..."

"I know what I want to do."

Bright morning sunlight filtered through the sheers and onto the tumbled blue satin duvet.

Dan looked up. Wrapped in a plush terricloth robe, he looked a little too casual for the circumstances.

Rose sipped a fresh cup of coffee and settled back on the window-seat. "I'm going to find Sir John."

"The guy with the castle?"

"That's right. How hard can it be to find a castle? The whole country's only that big. Somebody's got to know where Glen Diath is."

"Oh, I don't know if that's such a good idea, Rose."

She turned to him. "Why not?'

He shoved his hands into the pockets of his robe and hesitated. "Well, it's been a long time. You were just a kid then. Things might not be as attractive as you remember them."

She almost sloughed off his warning, then saw something else behind his eyes. "Dan, what are you afraid of?"

"Me? Nothing...I just don't want you to be disillusioned, that's all."

"Why do you think I'd be disillusioned?" She approached him critically. "Do you know something I don't know?"

He blinked and said, "Do I look like a castle spy to you?"

Surveying him with hands on hips, she said, "Well...you don't fit that motif very well, I guess."

Dan strode away a few steps, turned back. "Call the guy if you want to."

Suddenly the chance became a challenge. Rose reached for the phone and rang Information, all the while eyeing Dan. He was standing a few feet away, deliberately not showing any expression. She'd seen that stance, that look, before, though usually around the negotiation table. It seemed somewhat out of place in a hotel suite strewn with curling rose petals.

Jogged from her surveillance of Dan by the operator's voice, Rose quickly responded with, "Yes, I need help finding a residence, please. Well, that's the problem—I don't know. His name is Sir John Henwoodie. H-e-n-w...yes. He lives in a castle about an hour and a half drive from Glasgow, maybe two. Yes, I realize that's most of Scotland. Pardon? Oh, that's a good idea. Thank you. I'll do that." She hung up and pulled out the telephone book, glancing up at Dan to say, "Library."

Dan nodded, folded his arms, and his expression still controlled. Why didn't he want her to visit the castle?

Rose fought back an ominous chill as she rang up the library and had them trace Sir John through the Scottish Registry of Historical Buildings and Residences. Sure enough, there was a listing. Rose's heart started thumping as she jotted down the number. There was something nervewracking about those first few moments after the decision to phone an old friend, especially when the "old" meant going back over a decade, and stirring up so many memories of the one person they had in common—Red MacKenzie.

And making her even more nervous as she dialed was the sudden emotional distance from Dan. He watched her from scolding eyes, as if to say there was something he disapproved of, something that might hurt her—and him. Rose knew what she was sensing; she'd sensed it before. But always in the corporate office...never in the field of the heart.

Her hopes sank when a female voice answered the phone.... "Good morning, Castle Diath."

Rose hesitated, then forced herself to speak. "Hello? Is this still the residence of Sir John Henwoodie?" She held her breath, certain the woman would say no, that the previous owner was long gone.

"Yes, it is," the woman said. "May I say who's phoning, please?"

Rose's hopes sprang right up again and nearly choked her.

"Oh! Wonderful! Would you please tell him that...well, tell him it's Rose MacKenzie. If he doesn't remember, I guess that'll tell me everything I need to know."

"I see," the woman said, her clipped Scots twitter hovering somewhere between stern and pleasant. "Just one moment, then."

Rose's hands were cold and clammy. She glanced at Dan again, but he wasn't sharing her excitement—in fact, he was rather dampening it. Her glance became almost a glare as she rose to the challenge she sensed from him. Why was he looking at her like that?

"Rosie?" came a bellow through the phone. "Rosie Mack, is that you yourself in the skin?"

"Sir John?" Rose blurted, "You remember!"

"Remember! Huch, did you think I'd forget, you wee twig of a lass! Where are you?"

"Glasgow, but that can be—"

"The tatties are on the stove. You'll be late for tea if you don't fly! I'm dustin' off the ramparts and rakin' the shore for your visit. Bring ten or twenty friends and we'll turn loose!"

Rose let out a squeal of pure delight, turned suddenly eleven years old again. "This is unbelievable!"

"Well, you'd believe it if you'd been the one trying to keep tatties and herring fresh on the stove for near ten years since the last time you were here!. Walk oot the door, girl, what's the rrrrrush!"

"I'm walking! Give me directions."

"Directions! Why a blind coo cud sniff her way here in a snowstorm! Rule one, get a map."

"Got one."

"Go north out of Glasgow, up to Invergarry, hang a Louie."

"Louie. Got it."

"Swing on aroon' tee Bun Loyne."

"Bun Loyne."

"Another Louie."

"Louie the Second."

"Rin right along Loch Cluanie intee Glen Shiel on the Old Military Road—"

"Oh, I remember that!"

"Gae on to Loch Duich, hang a north, and you'll trip over the castle."

"Say no more," Rose laughed. "I remember...by gosh, I really do. We're on the way! Sir John, have you still got your beard?"

"Have I? Why, m'own mither'd niver recognize me wi'oot it! Ha' else would the dog know whae t'follow home?"

"Then I'm hurrying even faster," Rose said, actually giggling now. "Clear the grounds!"

"I'm pootin' the tea on!"

It was all they could do to hang up. Rose bounded to her feet and clapped her hands like a kid at a circus.

"He remembers! We've got to go! He's expecting us! I've got to rent a car!"

"I'll rent the car," Dan said calmly, apparently over his earlier disapproval. "You go get dressed. Can't be late to a castle, you know."

"Right! I'll get dressed! You rent the car!"

"Go." He nudged her toward the bathroom and picked up the phone. When the operator answered, he said "Would you connect me with the nearest car rental service, please? Something plush."

Rose clutched the piece of paper with Sir John's phone number on it as though it was a page from a special diary she didn't want to let go of, pressed it to her chest, and bounded into the bathroom. Dan could hear her singing as the shower turned on: "Happy days are heeeere again..."

There was a click on the other end of the line and a voice spoke, "Executive Auto...Jean speaking."

"Yes, I'd like to arrange for the best car on your lot..." Dan paused and waited for the sound of the water to go muted as a body stepped under it. Then he murmured, "Listen, I'll call back in a minute, okay?"

"Certainly, sir, as you wish."

Dan immediately got the operator again.

"Yes, would you ring a number for me quickly, please?" he asked, watching the bathroom door and lowering his voice. "John Henwoodie, Castle Diath, Dunan Dairmid. It's an Invershiel exchange. Yes, I'll wait."

Rose remembered Sir John Henwoodie very well. He was sixty-four feet tall, built like stacked barrels, his face was on fire, and he had coconuts for eyes and a row of machetes for teeth. Whe he laughed the walls crumbled. When he yelled, the towers caved in. Red MacKenzie called him Johnny Lionheart when they were drunk and Johnny Cope when they were mad at each other.

And Castle Diath...Hardly more than a relic when Sir John bought it some twenty-five years ago, the stone ruin had been on its way to becoming fairly livable when Rose visited as a child and a young teenager. The main hall and three bedchambers had been restored, the broken walls restoned and hung with tapestries, plumbing and heating installed, electricity wired in. Outside it had been still a relic, but that had been part of its charm. The main and lesser baileys were big gaps of ground surrounded by walls, colored only by the relentless Scottish moss. The big bailey extended halfway to the Near East, and the ramparts were ten cars across. There had been dragons roaring out of every crevice and fair maidens dropping long braids out of every tower window.

There it was!

Rose stood right up in the rented convertible Mercedes and shook her fists in the air. The castle glowered down at their approach as if to say, "Wha' bloody took yae sae lang?"

Rose peeled off her cashmere scarf and shook her hair in the wind blowing off Loch Duich. "Waaaaaaaoooooooow! she yelled at the rambling castle nestled among the crags.

"Shhh," Dan warned, glancing at her with a grin. "Remember your dignity, my dear." His glance shifted quickly back because driving on this skinny excuse for a road took all his attention. The road was paved—kind of—and it was just the width of the car.

"Oh, why didn't I come back when Gran was alive?" Rose called to the sight before her.

"Don't fill yourself up with those kinds of regrets, Rose," Dan suggested from beside her as she dropped back into the leather seat. His tone was lighter than his words, but his point got across.

"Maybe," she answered. "Maybe I've let too much slip by already."

"You sound negative," he observed.

She shrugged. Suddenly she was glad he was here beside her, and she wished they could take the nip off the anticipation with a quick tumble in the heather.

"I don't mean to," she told him.

Suddenly her voice was roughened by thoughts of him lying beside her in the wild grass on the lochside beside the castle. They could walk on the ramparts with no clothes on, stimulated by the offshore breeze, Scotland's smoky sky their wedding veil.

Secretly she hoped the medieval surroundings would give her a chance to erase the rude things she'd said to him in the past and earn his trust, so she would be free to trust him also. His glances welded her to desire now. He had made that reaction normal to her, and it wasn't going to go away. She loved him. He loved her. They were nirvana afire in bed together. She longed to feel his legs entangled with hers again. The desire was almost constant now.

On top of the desire, though, there was being with Dan. That experience in itself had begun to steadily enthrall her. When she was away from him, she longed to be with him again. Even while she showered, she couldn't wait to get out and be with him again. When had that change come over her?

The damnable part was that she no longer had any control over it—this joy in having him present.

She shook off her erotic thoughts and scanned the rocky countryside. "I see why my grandfather always talked so fondly of this country. You know, as a child I didn't really appreciate it."

"You look beautiful against it," Dan said softly, maneuvering the car over a rickety little bridge.

"Do I?" Rose was delighted. She looked down at the skin-tight designer jeans and the lightweight green cashmere pullover. She held up her hands and wiggled her fingers at him. "Nope. I lose half a point for a broken thumbnail."

Dan peered critically at her thumb. "Right. You only qualify as a nine-pointer. Sorry. Get out."

His mouth widened into a sensual smile. For a long moment the car slowed as he looked at her instead of the road, recovering barely in time to hug a curve. A tall crag loomed up before them, blocking their view of the ramparts.

Rose's throat tightened at that sultry caress of his eyes. She longed to be at the castle, high in a private tower, alone with him.

The car came around the crag and drove through the big gargoyled stone barbican attached to the castle gate and that had once been a wall around the main structure. Castle Diath rose before them like Emerald City—only gloomier. Rose actually gasped and pressed back against the leather seat.

"Damn," Dan chuckled, also affected by the sudden sight.

The castle's massive stone front was dominated by huge wooden doors with bronze ramshead knockers. The outer walls had been sandblasted back to their original gunmetal gray instead of sooty black, leaving sparkling masonry where once there had been only time-darkened grit.

Dan pulled the Mercedes up near the doors and parked. He got out and came around to Rose's side just as she climbed from the car, hypnotized.

He coiled an arm around her. "Inspiring," he murmured.

"Isn't it?" she whispered back. "It looks a lot better than when I saw it last. See those stained glass windows? They used to be just holes."

"Do you know how old the castle is?"

"Thirteenth century, I think."

"That's pretty old."

"I'd say. Sir John's a very determined man, to get it looking like this."

"From what you've told me, he probably wrestles down live elk for his breakfast. You sure he's the same species I am?"

Rose laughed. "I haven't figured out what species you are yet!"

"Oh, yeah?"

"Good comeback, Dan. I'm impressed."

"I'll impress you," he threatened, swinging her around into his arms, and caressing the soft places on her sides. His thumbs toyed with the tender outer swells of her breasts beneath the cashmere. He felt the lacy patterns of her bra and had to fight off the inclination to run his hands under the sweater.

She swayed against him, then recovered. "Dan! Not here!"

He waved one arm to take in the medieval setting and its natural romance, and echoed, "Not here?"

"Well, here," she said, "but not *yet*!"

"Halloo!"

They both turned just as the castle door swung open.

"Rosie!"

Rose broke away from Dan. "Sir John!"

It wasn't until the brazen gray-blond Santa Claus met her in a great bear hug that Rose realized he was actually shorter than herself by at least three inches. Funny how he'd shrunk. His eyes still had that flicker, though, and his laugh still bounced off the castle as though he did its breathing for it.

"Rosie, you're tall as a sapling and twice as supple!" Sir John bellowed, holding her at arm's length.

"It's you!" Rose cried. "It's actually you!"

"Why, 'course it's me! The old place and I are mossy as ever, fur sure. The castle's got a facelift and I'm just getting raggedy. B'god if you don't look the spittin' likeness of Red MacKenzie himself. 'Cept you're pretty and I'll bet you're softer tae the touch! Lookit you! If you're not a lady and a half!"

Rose laughed, overcome with delight, and reached for Dan's hand. "Sir John, I want you to meet someone." Oh, if only she could be introducing Dan to her grandfather...

"Never mind," Sir John said, surveying Dan with a keen eye. "I recognize'm."

Rose blinked. "You do?"

"Sure! He's the reincarnation of Rob Roy! Who else?"

Dan blushed, then stuck out a hand in greeting. "Dan Masters. How are you?"

"I'm perfect, as usual," Sir John roared, pumping Dan's hand.

Rose took a breath to say something, but a strange sound from the end of the driveway tickled her memory, and she turned. Two wiry gray faces came bounding toward her, paws spraying gravel everywhere. Deerhounds, at full tilt.

Gasping in surprise, Rose squealed, "This can't be Dundee!"

"Can and is," Sir John said. "Fifteen years old this month. The other one is Chance, Dundee's puppy by a good neighbor. She's almost ten herself."

The deerhounds ran into Rose's legs and climbed up her, encouraged by her laughter and attempts to rub both their funny narrow faces at once.

"Here now!" Sir John bellowed, intervening in the attack of passion. "Down with you both, y'great morons! Is this any way to behave? Down or I'll see your hides hanging on the wall by sundown! Crrretins!"

"They're all right," Rose said, pampering the two wiry gray faces.

"In fact, they fit right in! What would a glowering Scottish castle be without a pair of hounds?"

"There you've got me," Sir John huffed, fingering his thick blond-gray beard.

A teenage boy, with the red hair and freckled face of so many Scots highlanders, appeared and Sir John directed him to "take the coach around." The boy got the keys from Dan without a word, jumped in to the car, and drove it around the castle, evidently to some parking area that hadn't been there when Rose last visited more than a decade ago. The car had scarcely disappeared when a tiny white-haired woman with a tangled accent appeared and demanded to know if tea was wanted, when, and what with. Sir John barked back at her, and a truce was struck for tea in the living room in ten minutes.

No sooner was the woman gone than other servants also appeared, wanting to know which guest rooms would need preparing and so on, then just as quickly vanishing. Then the three of them were alone again, like main characters in a ghost story who'd just had a visitation.

"I don't remember all those people," Rose commented.

"Cuz they're new," Sir John popped back.

"Where do you find so many out here in the middle of nowhere?" Dan asked. "Most people have enough trouble finding good employees in a city."

"They all live hereabout," Sir John said, turning to Dan as he stood with his shoulders braced against the loch breeze. "All but two were unemployed, having a rough go all 'round, so I scooped'em up and put'em to the coals. Hamish, that skinny lad, goes to college up in Inverness. I'm putting him through, so he works for me on the side. Old Mrs. Gillespie, may she rot in perdition, was supported by her son until he died. That was when I hauled her over here and she pays her own way again. And wasn't it like pullin' a dragon out of its hole, too! It all works out, except that she prattles something fierce and I'm plotting to soon kill her in the night."

"Sir John," Rose said sincerely, "I had no idea I'd like you so well."

John put on a great offense and blustered, "And you didn't when you were wee?"

Rose laughed. "You scared the hell out of me then!"

"Shame on me. What say we repair to the lair?"

Rose laughed again and took his arm, glancing back at Dan, hoping he wasn't too offended by her choice of escort. He shook his head, grinned, stuffed his hands in his pockets, and sauntered after them.

What substance lay within as they strode through the wooden doors. Leather furniture in a deep oxblood brown and studded with brass hobnails, dominated the main living room. On the furniture were tossed lap robes and blankets in deep raw red, black, and green tartans that came crashing forward out of Rose's past. And she remembered them by clan name! This one was Gunn, that one Drummond, the rug was Black Watch Regimental tartan, and the ottoman was...well, three out of four wasn't bad.

It all looked like the cave of some slumbering mythical beast. Rose practically inhaled it.

Here was Sir John's Derbyshire tobacco box...and there was his collection of walking sticks, some more ornate than any walking stick had any business being. A French writing desk, topped with tooled hunter green leather backdropped by curtains in dark green and plum paisley that gave a heftiness to the room. Dark hardwood floors, wooden beams, and a brick fireplace that had been sandblasted clean gave the place anchor. Worsted fabrics were everywhere, including the covering of the muscular wooden day bed that reposed in a big bay window. Rose noticed that this window was new here, even though it fit together so well with what had been that she couldn't really separate new from old. One thing was certain: the castle's interior had taken a marked move toward the plush from the musty beginnings she remembered. It had a strong flavor of Scottish authenticity, right down to the round Jacobite targe and its accompanying broadswords hanging on one wall. Also on display was a black velvet doublet and a kilt in a tartan Rose didn't recognize. Apparently Sir John had taken a fancy to preserving such things.

She started to turn again to her grandfather's old friend, but as she did, light streaming in from a tall window danced over a graceful statuette.

Flora MacDonald. The delicate porcelain eyes still looked out over the loch, watching the tiny boat that carried Prince Charlie

Stuart away to safety on Skye. Her complexion was ruddy with the evening chill. Her skirts still swept gently into the loch wind, her tartan shawl fallen off one shoulder and hanging draped against her back.

She waited to be touched.

Dan watched Rose as she gazed across the long elegant room, and he gazed at the woman. No statue would ever match Rose MacKenzie in the eyes of the man who loved her. After a moment, he forced himself to look away from the breathtaking sight of her, and found Sir John looking at him. The two men, standing silently in the background during Rose's communication with the tiny figure, exchanged their own message.

Sir John nodded and tilted his head toward the statue.

Rose moved forward, one single step.

"Oh..." she sighed. "Flora..."

"Go ahead, lass," Sir John said. "She's been waiting for you all these years."

Rose hesitated, took another step, then held up one hand. "Would you mind if I..."

"Touch her?" Sir John completed. "Why not? After all, she's yours now."

In New York—back in his office against doctor's orders—Phil, almost put himself back in the hospital diving for the phone when his secretary told him McCall was on the line.

"Mac! What is it? What've you got?"

He listened for a long time. His expression changed so many times, he gave himself a headache.

When he spoke, his voice was a terrible scratch.

"Mac...that's the ugliest thing I've ever heard."

Chapter Twelve

SHE COULD HAVE believed in reincarnation as her hand drifted down the silken glass shawl of Flora Macdonald. She felt the presence of the moist moors, and felt a sense of other life in her, as though she'd lived here before, walked those marshes and stood upon the fog-brushed crags, looking out toward something that mattered to her. Though she couldn't see the landscape through the purple darkness from the balcony of her castle room, her memory of it was rekindled, her imagination fired by glimpses through the clouds. There was a beauty, primitive, erotic, about the land.

Her imagination put Dan back in time, too. In a kilt that swung around his bare knees and clung with its heavy leather straps to his bare waist. Only a draped plaid hung over his left shoulder, leaving his right shoulder and chest bare, his right arm free to swing the broadsword. His sandaled feet were buried in wildflowers, his left hand loosely gripping the bridle of a huge horse. His face was framed by a full golden beard, his hair a riot of uncombed, uncut yellow curls.

Rose felt her stomach knot with excitement at the idea of such barbarism on a loose leash. She liked the image of him that way, as different as it could be from the reserved man who'd strode into her life, holding the blue rose. Dan seemed to fit all aspects of her desires.

Even here and now.

She went out on to the loggia of her room, one of several that had been restored since she visited as a college student. From here she could see the clouds change color over the loch. The room itself, different from the others that had survived the centuries with the main structure, was an oriel, a room that extended out from the main building like a balcony. A big opium bed crawled across a Persian rug—evidently Sir John was a man of intercontinental tastes. Rose sat alone, caressing *her* statue and reveled in the anticipation of Dan's joining her.

Time between lovemaking had become like foreplay in itself. Everything from touch to glance had become a sensual blend. He'd be here soon. Rose vowed to hang on, to face the tide until she could draw him into her without any worries. She promised victory to the woman inside, the one Dan had found and stroked.

She could almost hear him.

"Beautiful night."

Rose touched Flora again as the porcelain rested in her lap, and only then realized that she hadn't imagined his voice after all. She turned.

"Beautiful woman, beautiful night," he said. He stood at the French doors, wearing only his dark blue undershorts and an unbuttoned shirt.

"I didn't hear you come in," Rose said.

He smiled. "I didn't. I just materialized like a wisp. I'm a ghost, remember?"

"Oh," she sighed, then, "You took your pants off."

For a moment he was silent. She couldn't see his face well, silhouetted as it was by the gentle lamplight from within. "Didn't you want me to?" he asked.

Rose let him worry for a playful count. Huskily she admitted, "I wanted to do it."

If he ever loved her, he loved her then.

Rose continued to study him. At this moment he was very nearly the man of her imagination. Dust-gold curls peeked through the open shirt, and there was a barbaric symmetry in the shape of his body. She ached with the dream of having his body and his love without the complexities that came with them, longing to trust him as much as she wanted to make love to him. She reached out and touched him.

He drew her closer.

"I'm glad to be here," she murmured, leaning into his embrace, "with you."

Elation rose in him, and he caressed her. Together they looked out over the seascape of Loch Duich. The water had a creeping fog for a petticoat tonight. The air was heavy with mist, but not enough to blur the view.

"There's a monster out there you know," Rose murmured against the curve of his shoulder.

"Sure there is."

"Just like the one in Loch Ness," Rose added playfully.

"Believe that, do you?"

"Would I be Scottish if I didn't?"

"A straightforward, contemporary, postrenaissance woman of the nineties believes in sea monsters?"

"Do you believe in whales?" she asked.

"Of course."

"Ever seen one?"

"Nope."

"There you go."

Dan laughed and rocked her gently in his arms. "Folkloric compost and you know it."

She turned and raised her brows at him. "It is not. There's a good hypothesis that a family of plesiosaurs is inhabiting the North Sea. So there."

"Oh yeah?" Dan breathed heavily. "You make my plesio soar."

"Hey," Rose warned, "no man speaks dirty to me." She coiled her arms around his neck and trapped his ears in the crooks of her elbows. "But I could learn to love it."

"Really?" Dan rolled his eyes and tried to look lewd. "Filth, obscenity, filth, sex, pet, filth, grind, thrust, lips, teeth, tongues—"

The balcony warmed to the sound of Rose's laughter. "I do love it!"

She laughed again as he bent down and lathered her neck, her ears, her shoulders with warm, wet kisses.

He drew back, searched inside his loose silk shirt, and said, "This is for you."

He drew out a short stem, and a perfect—if a bit wrinkled—rose bloom. Blue, of course.

Rose smiled. "Now, I know you didn't just pick this out of Sir John's backyard."

"Nope," he said. "Had 'em brought over by jet, just so I could continue making a hell of a good impression on you."

"Mmmm... Dan?"

"Yes?"

"How do you make them blue?" She sniffed at the lovely bloom, then rolled it gently along her cheek. "Do you put dye in the vase or something?"

Dan nearly choked. "If only!"

"How, then?"

"Well," he began, "you may not realize it, but you're looking at about four million dollars worth of molecular biology."

"Four *million*? Dollars?"

"And years of genetic research." He took the rose from her and touched its petals one by one with just the tip of a finger. "Some pollinating insects can see blue, but if there ever was a blue rose—and at least one ancient text says there was—the trait evolved out a long time ago. Rosarians have been cross-breeding for centuries, trying to get a true-blue rose. Closest they've come is a kind of lavender."

"I've seen those," Rose said. "It's almost silver. But it's not like this."

"I know. A Japanese company and an Australian lab have put a bundle into isolating the dormant enzyme for blue pigment, then tracing it back to the gene. The pigment's called 'delphinidin,' and it's—"

"Don't tell me. It makes delphiniums blue."

"And violets and irises, right. Then they spliced the gene into a bacterium, and infected the plant tissue at the cellular level. Neat, huh?"

"Neat enough to make me cross-eyed. Kind of takes the romance out of the rose," she said.

He turned to her. "Really?"

Slowly he drew the blue rose along her shoulder. It shot the mercury up on her thermometer, making her legs tingle until she couldn't fight the heat he stoked in her. Her head lolled back, giving him space, and he drew her down onto the carpet just inside the French doors. Touching him was like touching quicksilver—hot, electric, electrifying. Her clothing fell away beneath his hands and she luxuriated in her sudden bareness before him. This was going to feel so good...

Dan filled the sky. He was standing over her, straddling her hips like the Colossus of Rhodes over the canal. His body was silhouetted against the lamplight, a red glow curling around the edge of his limbs, shining on the muscles of his thighs, quivering on his arms.

"I have to have you, Rose," he whispered, his breath ragged, his fists clenched, his lips trembling and flavored with perspiration. "Now."

Rose smiled. This was the ultimate infection, this distant foreplay, neither touching the other, but engorged with looking, with the prophecy of the next half hour.

The rose dropped to the floor. Dan lowered to his knees. Her body responded in obvious hope. Her breasts swelled, her lips tingled, her breathing grew husky, her legs stiffened, her stomach tightened, her eyes glazed.

But there was no glazing over the way she took him. Her hands worked cleanly on his warm legs. She called out his name in crisp alarm as his kisses streamed over her breasts, quickening with the urgency of a locomotive gaining speed. Arousal yanked at her, but Rose fought it. She wanted it to be conscious, drawn out. She let herself fantasize about the ancient Highlander Dan might have been in a different age, exploring his thighs as though she was going up under that kilt she'd seen in her mind. When she had praised his body into perfect form, Dan took over. He lifted her tenderly to her knees before him, cupping her buttocks as she cupped his, and they came into each other in a union that mere days ago would have been unimaginable. They traded excitement for excitement, until the chimes rang loud and glorious and he sent her spiraling upward. There on the plush carpet they became a new constellation —the Lovers. They rocked away their need.

When the spiraling slowed and finally began to fade, Rose drowsily came to realize they were still on their knees, pressing into each other. She opened her eyes and found Dan's face in the dim lamplight.

"Dan," she whispered, pressing hot fingers to his cheeks.

"Wait," he murmured. "A few more seconds."

She closed her own eyes and let her shoulders drop back against his arms, feeling the chilly kiss of loch breeze on her bare body. The whole world was dim purple blue.

Jealous, the moon pulled a cloud over its face and went to sleep.

Rose awakened the next morning alone in the huge opium bed, its red coverlet tumbled all around her in an abandon that mimicked her night with Dan.

He was gone.

But his proxy was in place: the perfect blue rose bloom in repose on the pillow beside her. She smiled at it affectionately, and remembered the days when she had hated the sight of those roses.

No more, and never again.

Dan and Sir John were waiting for her on a brand new veranda extending out from the library. Breakfast was being served by cheerful locals who were sternly supervised by Mrs. Gillespie. Mrs. Gillespie wasn't happy with anything, but the two locals had apparently become adept at ignoring her without hurting her feelings. They were muttering, "Yes, Mrs. Gillespie" and "Right away" with the expertise of a bored husband.

Rose drifted out onto the veranda, feeling beautiful. She and Dan exchanged an immediate, sensually knowing look of intimacy so obvious that Sir John quickly looked out onto the loch and surveyed it as though he'd never seen it before.

Rose sat down beside Dan and found herself suddenly being served eggs, ham, and shortbread. She couldn't drink the tea faster than the staff would resupply it, steaming hot.

"Sleep well, Rosie?" Sir John asked.

"Better than well," she responded. "I feel like I've come home."

She gazed at Dan. She swelled with gratitude that he had persisted in trying to awaken the woman within her, the one who could actually love him.

He grinned, but said nothing.

Sir John flicked a crumb off his beard and said, "How 'bout gathering wildflowers or some other female preoccupation this morning while I show Dan what fishing on a loch is like, eh?"

Rose sipped her tea and accused, "Oh? You want to go off and man around, do you? Just assuming a woman can't handle a live worm, are you?"

"Nope," Sir John told her. "I remember you aren't too fond of fishing."

"You've got me there," she admitted. "I never really took to it, did I?"

"You sat in the boat and growled at Red the whole time. I didn't figure you'd fish for anybody else if not for him."

She nodded with nostalgia. "Okay, you guys go off and try not to come back smelling of wet weeds and scales."

"It's a promise," Dan said emphatically. He leaned over the table and kissed her. "Thanks."

"Is that a woman's woman, or what!" Sir John bellowed.

"That's a woman," Dan murmured, glowing with pride.

They left later that morning, leaving Rose agleam with Dan's affection. She felt as though she was swimming in love for him, and it kept her feeling light all day.

All day, until the telephone rang in the main hall. Mrs. Gillespie appeared at the library door.

Rose looked up from the magazine on interior design she'd found on Sir John's desk.

"There's a telephone call for you, miss," Mrs. Gillespie cackled. "Long distance from America."

Rose smiled at how these words sounded with the Scottish accent. "Thank you. This phone?" She pointed to an antique designer phone on the desk.

"Oh, aye, miss, that's the one."

"Thank you," she repeated. The old lady disappeared, closing the library door behind her as Rose picked up the receiver. "Rose MacKenzie."

"Hi..."

"Phil? Is that you?"

"Yes, it's me. Sorry."

A cold sensation came over Rose. She knew that tone.

"Is something wrong?" she asked.

"Well...how are you guys doing? Having a good time?"

"We're having a wonderful time," she said, knowing she'd have to get the pleasantries out of the way before she got straight answers out of him. "Sir John's got this old castle looking like a piece of artwork."

"Be sure to tell him I said hello, if he even remembers me."

"He does. He asked about you yesterday at dinner. I don't think he's ever forgotten anything in his whole life."

"Well, that's great."

"Phil?"

"Yes?"

"Are you going to tell me or am I going to have to come through the phone line?"

There was a silence on the other end now, and the feeling of coldness deepened. She thought she heard a sigh, and not one of relief.

"Rose..."

Rose steeled herself. It couldn't be that bad. Dan just couldn't be that bad.

"Give it to me, Phil. I mean it."

"It's an inheritance restriction," he said.

"Inheritance!" Rose blurted. "Mine or his? What are you saying?"

"I'm saying—as weird as it sounds—that Dan is subject to an inheritance restriction that says he has to marry Rose MacKenzie before...before the age of forty."

Phil breathed heavily, as though he'd run a mile. He had thought it would feel good getting down to the grist, but it didn't.

The grinding silence from Glen Diath was disemboweling.

"Where did you hear this?" Rose finally asked, stiffly.

Phil took a deep breath and spoke very slowly—he didn't want to have to say it a second time.

"One of McCall's investigators got a secretary to talk at an international probate law firm. The secretary and a few of the lawyers there have a bet going about whether or not the inheritance'll go through."

"It's just gossip then."

"Rose—" Phil stood up and paced. "It's *not* gossip. It is *not* a rumor. It's information. It's evidence. Names, descriptions, dates—it's a will, Rose. A will drawn in England, apparently. It mentions you by name. That's the link between the secretary and all the talk—How else would your name come up with Dan's? Listen to me. It's a legally binding inheritance to a London account that names Dan as its beneficiary, and you as a stipulation. There's no limit on how odd a person can be or what he can put in his will, short of murder—and that's been done, too. It's silly, it's tricky, it's eccentric, but it's legally ironclad...and binding on Dan." He paused, and finally got around to saying something they both wanted to hear. "It's not Dan who's crazy. It's whoever made out that damned will! That's why Dan seems so civil, and why all this seems to be bothering him. He's trapped, too."

Trapped. Rose started to shake. Her lips were suddenly dry, her skin tight.

"Now understand—it doesn't obligate *you* to anything," Phil added, "but it completely obligates Dan."

Rose wanted to babble all the typical phrases—was he sure, wasn't there some mistake, maybe it was all a joke—but she knew Phil better.

'Who..." She had to stop and swallow the lump in her throat. "Who wrote the will?"

"I don't know yet. Could be anyone in the past fifty years. I suspect it was someone who had a grudge against your grandfather. Some rich old codger wrote you into his will as revenge against Red MacKenzie. Or a grudge against Dan's grandfather—oh, hell, I just don't know yet. I'm so sorry,...I'm so sorry, Rose..."

The phone bill mounted and mounted. Rose sat there in grueling silence as Phil attempted useless comforts, even offered to come to Scotland to get her out of all this. But she just sat there, trying to soak it all in, trying hard not to blame Dan for someone else's grudge, then blaming him for not being honest, then wishing he weren't so good an actor, then damning him for being so kind...round and round she went, through pain, defensiveness, anger, and back...sympathy and back.

Phil kept asking if she was all right. She kept muttering yes, she would live through this. She would survive.

This wasn't a game. Dan was really trapped.

So how come my heart is the one that's bleeding?

"Phil," she croaked finally.

"I'm right here, Rose. Tell me what you want me to do."

"I want you to keep looking, find out if this is all there is to the story. You know, get the details—"

"Yes, I'll do it."

"Find out if this is something Dan's known about for a long time or what."

"Okay."

"And find out about the inheritance. Where's the money coming from... who wrote that will... what Dan's personal involvement is, then call me right back."

"All right." The shuffle of papers indicated that Phil was scribbling as well as he could with his good hand. "That's smart," he said. "He's got to have some appropriation rights on that money, or he wouldn't be throwing a couple hundred grand around on old cars like he did at the auction. Rose—"

"Hmmm..."

"You realize," he said slowly, "you can't marry him now, don't you? If you do, you'll always be wondering."

Rose thought of the little statue on her bedside table. Sad Flora, bidding goodbye to the Prince.

"I'll always wonder anyway," she whispered.

Chapter Thirteen

BEHIND THE SEMIRUINED walls of the main bailey, where once there had been only dust, was a garden. The lofty shapes of Irish yews towered almost to the height of the castle walls. Their shadow was welcome to Rose now. She'd really meant to go inside now that Dan and Sir John had returned, to talk to Dan, maybe find out if it was true, if Phil's information was accurate, his conclusions correct.

Rose was a quick study where the law was concerned, and she was troubled by her own perceptions.

She'd played over and over again how she would act, what she would say. She could pretend nothing was wrong. She could stall Dan. She could distract him as thoroughly as she herself had been distracted. She'd run dialogue back and forth in her mind, trying to practice how to keep him from knowing what she'd found out. But none of it sounded as convincing as it would have to be. The Rose MacKenzie who could play those games no longer existed. She was a different Rose now, one without thorns. All that remained was the confrontation—and the awful moment when she would have to leave him.

Now Dan had rubbed the patina off of her strength, leaving a hole just his size.

Love. It sounded so simple. Four little letters that liked to sing together.

Resentment could take the sheen off a good love. She sympathized with Dan—if the story was true—but Phil was right. She couldn't marry him now, knowing this.

She plucked at a bough of Irish yew and murmured, "I won't live like that, tree. I'd rather live with the memory of our love as it was yesterday. I need my self-respect more than a warm bed."

That last sentence sounded plenty shaky.

She walked away from the cold castle walls and down the brae to the loch shore. If not for the dim moon, it'd be impossible even to walk in this consuming darkness, for there wasn't a light anywhere.

She'd forgotten how dark the Highlands were. There was no darkness as black and forbidding and silent as that of the Highlands of Scotland. There was no comforting hum of distant traffic, no passing planes, no electrical wires, certainly no city lights. Not even the glow of a town on the horizon. Some of these glens didn't even get sunlight until the middle of March. It was utterly dark, utterly primitive.

Easy to see know ghost stories would come out of these narrow glens. Easy to see the impetus for Scotland's eerie folklore.

"Rose?"

She spun around.

Dan moved toward her. "What are you doing way down here?"

"How did you know I was here?" she countered. No matter how she tried, she couldn't keep the accusative sting from her voice.

He shrugged. "I saw you from the window. It's dangerous to walk around here at night."

"It's not dangerous," she said. "Not half as dangerous as some things."

Dan chuckled, perplexed. "What?"

"Nothing," she said.

He nodded, not believing her at all. "Uh-huh. Does this have anything to do with that phone call?"

"It was just Phil."

"How is he?"

"He's fine. Everything's fine."

"Okay . . ." Dan circled her, sensing her hostility enough to keep a little distance between them. "Am I sensing a void with my picture on it?" he asked slowly.

Rose turned fully to face him. She paused, adding to the tense silence that descended like a curtain between them. A breeze hummed softly. The melody was hollow.

"No," she said. "But there are a lot of questions that start with 'Dan.' I think I'm going to start asking some of them pretty soon."

His eyes narrowing in surprise, Dan took a shallow breath and said, "You've…caught me at a disadvantage. I thought we were doing all right."

"We were," she said.

"Then why all this?" He paused, then lowered his tone. "What did Phil tell you?"

"Never mind Phil for now. This is about us."

Dan held his arms out and rasped, "*What* about us? I have a feeling 'us' is in trouble again."

"I'm just tired of the mystery, Dan," Rose began, her neck prickling as it always did before she broached a challenge. As she gazed at his astonished face, devouring its handsome lines with her eyes, she lowered her voice and added, "It's time for me to know."

Water from the loch inched up around the soles of his shoes. It was as though he was trying to escape into the brine. He rubbed the length of his forefinger under his lower lip in a gesture of thoughtfulness, trying to decide if indeed it was her time to know. Would she understand? Had he found enough woman under the corporate executive to enable her to understand? Would she accuse him of defacing the perfection they'd found in their passions?

Those were frightening possibilities. They made him more nervous than the determination in her face now, the casual strength and womanhood in her body as she folded her arms under her loose breasts and waited for his explanation. She wasn't cowering. No, she wasn't the coward around here right now.

Rose watched Dan, carefully controlling her expression. She knew how to do that, but this time it took plenty of self-control. Dan had said he wanted to marry her—a marriage, not a merger.

Oh, Gran, why couldn't you be here so I could ask you what to do?

The thought of her grandfather suddenly weakened her, and she had to stand up a fraction straighter to make sure Dan didn't see the change.

His feet making squishing noises in the soft loch shores, Dan moved closer to her. His face hardened, his blue eyes iced over.

"I'm a flesh-and-blood man, Rose, not a tickertape machine for you to measure your success on."

"You enjoy playing me out at the end of your line," she shot back. "It's my turn to know things about you. It's my turn to see the light and you know it. Aren't you enough of a man to show all your colors?"

He pressed his lips tight and shook his head. "I thought we were done with this."

"Done?" Rose challenged. "What do you take me for?"

Dan whirled away, then back again, his body tight. "I can't believe I'm hearing this..."

Rose inhaled deeply to steady herself. She forced herself to stay in control even as she stoked the fire of her anger. Only anger would let her fight him now. She knew that if she looked into the eyes she so dearly loved without the strength of her anger, she would weaken. She'd been warned, but she'd let it happen.

Dan hesitated, a trapped expression flitting for a second across his face. His hand disappeared into his pockets as they always did when he was uncomfortable. "What do we do about this, Rose?"

"Easy. I listen, you talk."

He shook his head. "No deal."

Stalemate.

The loch licked the shoreline nervously. The tension grew. Dan mumbled something about seeing her back at the castle and began to walk away.

She watched him walk away with a boldness that said he wasn't ashamed of himself. Hollowness engulfed her. Rose discovered it was much worse than the emptiness of not being loved at all.

There had been a strength in his eyes as he had faced her that made her ache with hopeless love, made her want to lie back on his bed and warm his fog-cooled skin. But there was no stopping what she had to do, for her own sanity.

She could still see his fists curling into balls of frustration. She recalled the touch of his hands and almost cried out to him with the agony of knowing there would be no more touching. Even as she called up the anger again, her breasts swelled with a pitiful response to the strides he took as he walked away from her and grew small against the walls of the castle.

Her lips parted. She took the breath to call out to him.

The sound never came.

No matter. It would have been drowned out by her weeping soul.

"Call for you, Miss MacKenzie, in the main hall."

Rose jumped, even though she had been expecting the call. She wanted to bring Alexander Graham Bell back from the dead, then kill him.

"Phil?"

"Sure is."

"Tell me."

"You won't like it."

"Too late, Phil, I already don't."

"Remember you told me that Dan said he studied agriculture in England?"

"Yes..."

"Rose, it's Garden King. That's the source of the binding will, and the fortune Dan's sitting on."

Rose sat down slowly onto a tufted leather ottoman. "Garden King? Our contractors? Our greenskeepers? Our florist? Our agriculturists?"

"That's right. Good old Garden King, whom we've trusted for years. Dan Masters is the principal stockholder."

Stunned silence coiled around Rose. She couldn't even respond. She stared into the thick tartan rug at her feet.

Phil waited a few beats, reading her silence, then said, "It's no wonder we couldn't find him. He was hiding in our own back yard. I've traced the will back to a British counselor, who of course won't tell my anything about the stipulations in it, *but* we did a sweep on legal representation of American and English businesses, and we found Garden King is the common denominator. It was just a skip and jump from there to finding out about Dan's holdings in that company. Are you still listening?"

Rose nodded. When she realized he couldn't see her, she croaked, "Yes...go on."

She heard Phil take a deep, steadying breath, and knew that as quickly as he was talking and as efficient as he sounded, this was hard for him.

"Garden King," he went on, "owns a number of subsidiaries that have been buying up stock in MacKenzie since we went public six years ago."

"Oh, my God..."

"You're still the controlling stockholder, but if we add together all the stock Garden King now controls, it equals almost two-thirds as much as you own. They could challenge you, Rose. And I think that's what they're planning to do."

Rose's hands began to shake. She pressed the receiver so tightly to her head that her ear started hurting. "How could we have failed to notice this?"

"Because it's such scattered stock," Phil said. "They've always voted by proxy, and they've gone along with anything you've done. That way, they stayed inconspicuous. Who knows how long this has been fermenting? Dan's tied to that will, and maybe that's to blackmail him into controlling you, and into marrying you, so that his company could come in and take control of MacKenzie." He paused. "There's something more. Rose, Garden King has just applied for a substantial loan."

"A loan," Rose gasped. "Oh, God, Phil...if they go into the market and use that money to buy up more stock in MacKenzie—"

"You'll lose control. And Dan will have it."

Phil paused again, an ugly and regretful pause.

"You were right. He was distracting you so you could be blindsided. It's a takeover, Rose...it's a takeover."

Chapter Fourteen

"DEVELOPED A YEN for fog?"

Sir John's words were themselves almost lost in the cotton-thick mist that had descended around Diath. The ramparts were chilly summits now, one hardly visible from the other. The oldest portion of the castle, a circular keep on the opposite side from the main bailey, was totally out of sight.

Dan only half-turned. "And you couldn't sleep, I suppose."

Sir John Henwoodie pulled the collar of his cardigan up around his neck under the beard and said, "I come from a long line of folks who can't sleep when other folks in their castles are having tiffs. Family curse and all."

"What makes you think we're having a tiff?"

"Easy. She's inside. You're out here."

"Ah."

"Since you were that high, you've been stubborn as a pitbull," Sir John reminded him. "Fess up, Danny. You've screwed this one up all to bits."

Dan sighed. "I didn't exactly lie to her, John. I never have. I just haven't filled her in."

"Haven't filled her in on what, precisely? Wanna explain it to a curious soldier wi' no sense of propriety?"

With a chuckle, Dan said, "You old meddler. You can't stand not knowing the rest of the gory details, can you?"

"Nope."

"You're not going to like it, John. Red MacKenzie meant almost as much to you as he did to Rose."

She was alone in the world.

Her best friend was three thousand miles away. Her grandfather's best friend was somewhere on the grounds. The man who said he loved her was within reach.

But she was totally alone.

All she had was her strength, and that was a poor lifeboat.

The big clock on the wall bonged the hour. A deep, brassy noise. One...two...three...four...five...six...seven...

It was dark outside. Dark everywhere.

"Rose?"

Her throat knotted around any chance for response. How long had she been sitting here with the phone to her ear?

"Rose, I'm really sorry about all this," Phil murmured. "I liked him too."

She tried once again to clear her throat, and this time almost succeeded.

"What can we do about this?" she asked.

Phil sighed. "He's got a wide jump on us. He really bulldozed us in order to satisfy the legalities that are tying him up. I know he's trapped, but it bothers me that he wasn't just honest with you from the beginning. We could've tried to find some legal way out of his problem. He didn't have to try to trap you, too."

"He isn't aware that we know about this," she asked, "is he?"

"No, I don't think so. Why?"

"What's his percentage of ownership in Garden King?"

Phil was quiet a moment. He didn't like the change in her voice. He knew she was forcing herself to talk, but the words were clinical, harsh.

"Twenty-eight percent," he told her.

Rose's voice grew stronger as she allowed the outer woman to take command, to become a shell over the pain. "That's enough to control a corporation, but it's not indomitable. Garden King is public, isn't it?"

"Yes. His company grew so fasr that all he could do was go public. His control isn't absolute. Everything always goes his way, but it's no dictatorship."

Rose nodded, even though Phil was an ocean away. She knew he could sense her nod. It gave her comfort. As though Phil was closer.

"Here's what you do," she said carefully. "Create some paper investment companies in West Germany, London, Switzerland, and Hong Kong. Start quietly and quickly buying up stock in Garden King."

"Rose...I don't know..."

"When's their next board meeting?"

"Do you find it a coincidence that it's eight days from now?"

The pain went through her shell and stung her so hard she winced. Dan's timing became glaring evidence. She tightened her arms around her ribs and ground out her words.

"We can keep it quiet for eight days. I don't want him to know what's going on. It's still daytime in Hong Kong and San Diego. Get started as soon as we hang up. Approach the big investors in Garden King. Offer them twenty-five percent over the current value of their stock. Are you well enough to do this personally? I only want you and maybe two other people you trust implicitly. Charter jets and go around to these places yourselves over the next few days. You coordinate all the buys, but it has to be done anonymously. Don't tell them who's doing the buying. Wave twenty-five percent in front of these people, and they won't *care* who's buying. Report back to me by telex. We've got to save MacKenzie from outside control. It's a family company, Phil, *my* family."

Phil shifted uneasily. God, it was scary when she turned this way.

"What about Dan?" he forced himself to ask. "What about the bind he's in? That inheritance he's answerable to?"

"That's his problem," Rose said. The chill in her voice hurt them both. "I'm not going to let him make it mine."

Vengeance put dirt on her words. She heard it, and she knew Phil heard it. She had to summon all her professional armor in order to keep from screaming.

"Rose," Phil said, "get out of there. Get away from the castle. Get away from Dan. Don't let him see you leave. Don't look at him again. If you look at him...you'll melt."

"The will went into effect when Red MacKenzie died. I stalled as long as I could, but then I had to take action."

"Rosie won't like being the action."

"I know!" Dan said. "That's why I keep getting this voice in my head saying 'tell her, tell her and get it over with.'"

Sir John grunted. "The voice has more sense than you do. Don't you believe Rosie loves you yet?" the old man asked bluntly. His beard glistened as it picked up moisture from the fog. He stood there, washed in moonlight, looking like some old oracle come to life.

Dan's eyes narrowed to thoughtfulness, his face full of trouble. "She loves some part of me. She might only be here because I'm—"

"Stubborn as a pitbull?"

"Well... I don't know if stubborn tells it. Even if she loves me now, when she finds out all this, she's not going to love me anymore. And I'll lose everything, not just her. All because Red MacKenzie couldn't keep his pants on."

"Ah, you always were a pompous little toad, Dan, and all you are now is a pompous big toad. You win or lose in life. You can't straddle. Rose won't take that. She's not the kind of woman who wants half a man. I can see that already. She's got Red MacKenzie in her just as if he was still alive, and you can't fool that. Don't be so clatter-brained you can't deal with it. If I was ten years younger, I'd deck yeh."

Resisting the urge to run his hand along the wet stone rampart, just to see if he could still feel, Dan mused, "If you were ten years younger, I'd take you up on it. You're just a lamb in lizard's underwear and I know it."

He leaned over the rampart, looked through the shapes of the Irish yews, in hopes of catching another glimpse of Rose. But there was no lithe spectre anymore, no glint of moonlit auburn in the mist.

"She was so happy when we got here," he murmured. "Then she suddenly started hammering me with questions again. I thought she'd started to trust me."

"Dan! Screw your head on! You might as well tell her everything. What's the difference now anyway? It's not that complicated a story."

"I've already got a father, John. I don't need two." Only when the silence at his right shoulder met the silence from the country-side did Dan shake himself. Sir John was leaning on his castle like one old warhouse leaning on another. Dan managed a guilty smile and said, "Sorry, John."

"You're boneheaded too."

"Yeah, I know." Dan looked out over the dark land and sighed. "How can I tell her something like this about the grandfather she adored? The man whose business she's protecting? And...what's she going to think of *me*?"

"This is tawdry, Dan," Sir John told him, "and below you. Pull up your pants and stop thinking with your gonads. Forget she's a woman. Forget she's Rose MacKenzie. Forget she might be in love with you. Forget everything except how to talk. Get your ass into your bedroom and for your own sake forget there's a bed there. Talk to the girl, Daniel. You owe her."

It wouldn't have been so hard to hear if it hadn't been true. Dan rubbed his fists on the cold, sweating stone. Then he stood straight and stuffed them in his pockets. "I'm going inside. I've got better things to do than listen to your Bogart imitation."

"It's not Bogart. It's Mickey Spillane. You just didn't recognize it because of my accent."

Sir John watched with one eyebrow raised as Dan walked toward the outside stairway that led inevitably to Rose. Maybe he'd overstepped his place a half-hair, but youngsters needed a kick in the skivvies from time to time. He had had to use his heavy boots on Dan, but maybe it would do some good. If only the poor lad hadn't come to love the girl so much, none of this would be so hard.

"John?"

"Yep?"

"You shouldn't have been knighted." A breeze swirled between them. "You should've been sainted."

He rehearsed everything twenty times on his way back to their room. He paused a dozen times to see how it sounded in his head. John was right; it didn't sound like enough to keep silent about anymore. In fact, it was suddenly lost on Dan why he'd bothered to keep all this a secret in the first place. Nothing seemed to matter anymore, nothing but the fact that he was on the edge of losing Rose after finally having found her. Every time he tried to think rationally, though, he was dizzied by the lingering taste of her skin on his lips. The memory of last night made him lightheaded, made it hard for him to think of leveling with her, of losing the edge he'd been clinging to for so long. Rose had clung to him out of curiosity alone, he knew that—at least at first. Letting go of that last crumb he'd been dangling before her made him uneasy. But John was right. It was time.

He walked up the long staircase with his fingers afire. Even if she balked at his explanation, he would touch her as he had last night and she would melt against him again, knowing that the touch was real. It was far more real than the vague worries that had kept him from telling her about the legal straps that tied him to deals made before he was old enough to spell.

They had something together that would rise over that gulf. He forced himself to keep believing that as he stepped onto the landing and headed down the narrow corridor to the room he shared with Rose MacKenzie.

When she forgave him for everything and realized that all this had been a series of events he couldn't change, she would sway against him and kiss him, and he would kiss her back. Then he would draw her out on to the stone loggia overlooking the loch, and he would ask to be more than her lover. He would ask to be her husband.

Her husband...her husband...a dream come true for the boy who'd stood outside the tall glass walls of the Coachman and looked in at the lithe, striking granddaughter of the owner. He'd been attached to the MacKenzie family by tenuous threads all these years, all the time dreaming of one day being worthy of Rose.

Now he was worthy of her, and the gift of honesty was the next thing he would bestow.

He pushed the heavy door open.

"Rose?"

His voice was like a boom in the silence.

He stepped into the room, suddenly chilled. A funny feeling.

The blue rose lay at his feet. He almost stepped on it.

It hadn't been thrown there, just carefully placed where he would see it first thing. On the floor. A clear statement.

All her things were gone. The bed was made. The bathroom was empty. The loggia was cold.

She was gone.

Chapter Fifteen

SHE DISAPPEARED INTO the Scottish fog that very night.

Sir John's red-headed bellhop drove her to the nearest excuse for a town, where she used her considerable credit cards to arrange transportation...and silence. She couldn't cut a trail for herself in the forest, but she could bury one in any city. She had left a note for Sir John, thanking him and saying she was going to England for a few days. Needed to clear her head. And would he please entertain Dan for her...keep him occupied for a while? Maybe a week?

Phil's arm was aching. Hell, everything ached.

He was back in one of his silk suits, but that semblance of company life didn't help much. The black sling on his arm was making his neck ache, but when he took it off, his shoulder hurt too much. He couldn't win.

He wouldn't have any more chances to have Rose turn to him. If he wasn't strong enough to give her the emotional—and passionate—support she needed, this episode would make her so strong that she wouldn't need him or anyone to fill that place where love should reside. The victory of discovering who Dan was and why he had been acting the way he did—that was his anchor. Phil had hacked the hole out of the rock, but now he didn't know know to fill it. The idea of Rose coming home was nerve-wracking, not exciting, and not comforting. He couldn't even imagine putting his arms around her under these circumstances.

So he sat in his office, alone with his win.

Only the chirp of his office line made him move, and then only by force of responsibility.

"Yes?"

"Sir, there's a call for you from the Boston office," his secretary told him.

"I'll take it." He punched the blinking line and said, "Philip Van Dyke."

"Mr. Van Dyke, this is Don Stark in Boston."

"Yes, Don. What've you got for me?"

"I've got a to-the-hour report on D. Evans Masters and Garden King. Monies appropriated through the recent loan he applied for. I can FAX this to you."

"Great. Do that," Phil told him. "What's the bottom line?"

"Let me see...yes, here it is. I think this is going to make you very happy."

It was a typical board meeting. People in power suits, munching power Danishes, telling power jokes over executive coffee, around a long shiny black table that looked like it might drive away any minute.

Dan almost enjoyed it. These were people he'd know all his business life. People he liked, people he trusted. The very first investor, for one. And others who'd stuck their hands into the fire for him. He'd made sure they had all come out ahead, that Garden King grew as it was supposed to grow. Like a skyrocket.

Because of that, these meeting were more like family barbecues, and he always looked forward to them.

This morning especially, he needed to have friends around him. He knew they could see past his smiles and casual jokes to the pain that still lurked in his eyes, but they didn't know what predicated it, and they were polite enough not to ask. He was grateful for that. Rose had left him confused. He needed time to figure out how to get her back.

Maybe that was why he could still joke and banter. He knew she would be with him again. She loved him. He was sure of that. She couldn't have faked that look in her eyes, the shivering response that ran along her body at his touch. He'd been with women who had faked. There had been far more than seduction going on between them. She loved him.

Everything would come around.

He kept telling himself that. He took solace in the presence of old friends and partners and in the security of the company he'd built around himself. He only wished Red MacKenzie could be here to—

He saw her face. He saw her body. She was astonishing. Dressed in the shades of the castle—hunter green jersey, a paisley shawl over one shoulder, her slim waist caught in a brown leather belt, striding at her full height in high-heeled shoes...the sight left him breathless. Was he imagining her?

From his seat at the head of the table, Dan saw her as he might have seen a vision, striding in the middle door with a covey of attendants and lawyer types around her. Rose towered over them, even the three men among her entourage.

Rose MacKenzie's people spilled into the conference room, ignoring the gawks of Dan's company people. They had briefcases and ledgers and tape recorders.

"Rose!" Dan came slowly to his feet. "What's this all about?" he asked bluntly, addressing the whole group, but speaking to Rose, God, she was gorgeous, stunning...

And that was certainly the word to describe her effect on him. Stunned. Why was she here? And why now?

Perspiration broke out on the back of his neck at the sight of her. All his strength collapsed and gathered at the core of his loins. He ached to hold her and crush himself against her. She was magnificent in those clothes, and her demeanor was possessive of him.

She looked at him once, firmly, but only once. After that, she merely nodded to her people, and took one of the empty seats.

"Sit down, Mr. Masters," one of the female attorneys said. This woman also was stunning, a blond woman of about forty, dressed impeccably in flowing mahogany browns and maroons. Rose had succeeded in setting quite an example at her company's headquarters. When Rose MacKenzie and her associates entered a room, the room became vague and all others dimmed.

Dan felt himself dimming.

However, he wasn't pleased with being dimmed in his own

company headquarters. He not only remained standing, but took a step toward the attorney.

"Would you like to explain your presence at our board meeting, please?" he demanded.

"Yes, sir, I'm going to do exactly that," she said, quietly but not snidely. Perhaps that was part of her orders. "My name is Eleanor Bench, and I'm acting head attorney for MacKenzie and Family Enterprises and Royal Coachman International. Please..." She motioned toward Dan's chair.

Dan looked at Rose. She was whispering to one of her other associates. His own associates were looking at him. They were mystified—and nervous.

After a moment he gestured to Ms. Bench to begin, and slid onto the edge of his chair.

"Thank you," Ms. Bench said. "I have in my possession copies of stock reports, as of this morning, from Copenhagen...London and Dublin...Gstadt...San Diego...Paris...and Amsterdam. These reports specify ownership of shares in Garden King equalling no less than fifty-four percent of the total outstanding stock of the company—"

The room erupted. Dan's associates roared with indignation, demanding to know what this was all about. Ms. Bench held up one hand and patiently waited for silence.

Only Dan was unmoving, unspeaking. He simply stared at Rose. The only change was a slight loss of color from his ruddy cheeks.

Ms. Bench gave the room a perfect schoolteacher's I'm-waiting look, and finally continued.

"On behalf of MacKenzie and Family Enterprises, Incorporated, and Royal Coachman International, Incorporated, I announce the controlling purchase of this company and the dismissal of its leadership until further notice. The new Board of Directors will be selected at a later date, as approved by the primary stockholder, Miss Rose MacKenzie."

Again the room exploded. This time the Garden King board came to their feet almost as a single entity, vowing everything from lawsuits to vengeance.

Rose remained still, surrounded by her people. She gazed down at the glossy black table. In it, at the far end, she saw the reflection of Dan Masters. He was pain itself.

Her pain. Her very own.

Only when someone turned in desperation to Dan and demanded that he do something about all this did the room quiet down. Everyone was waiting to see what the now former president had to say. Dan would take care of it. Dan would fight this.

But they also knew that he couldn't fight it. A takeover by a company as powerful as MacKenzie simply couldn't be fought. Even if it could, the fight would take years. There wasn't even time for a beginning today. They could see now that the battle was going on right here before them—between Dan Masters and Rose MacKenzie. It was a devastating one. It raged in that barely visible region behind Dan's eyes, sending out a crushing look that transferred his pain to Rose as effectively as circuitry.

Her own fingers clawed into the cushion of her chair. His hurt, his fury, contained in a pressure cooker of human sinew, roused the same womanly needs in her as his desire had mere nights ago. He was standing maybe twelve feet from her, but he might as well have been pressed against her, pelvis to pelvis.

He stared at her in unanswered silence.

The room grew silent as everyone waited for Dan to say something.

The pall of shock over Dan Masters would've melted any brick wall and left nothing but a puddle of empathy. His patriot-blue eyes, now widened in astonishment, stared not at Ms. Bench, but at Rose MacKenzie. His hands were white. His cheeks were like paper. Clearly he was more dumbfounded than anyone else.

"Mr. Masters," Ms. Bench began, her voice lowered substantially, "we're interested in a smooth changeover. We hope you'll—"

He stood up slowly. His eyes never left those of Rose MacKenzie.

All at once it was as though he and Rose were completely alone in the room. He held out a hand toward her. His voice was no more than a breath.

Softly he murmured, "Why?"

Not a dime.

Not one red cent.

Phil sat in his office, staring at the still-warm document that had just come off the FAX machine. He'd never been so baffled. Everything, absolutely everything, had pointed to Dan Masters' moving to take control of MacKenzie and Family Enterprises as soon as that big loan came through.

So... why hadn't he?

Dan could've take over, then blackmailed Rose into that marriage deal.

There it sat, right in front of him. Solid proof of Dan's innocence. Garden implements in Europe. That's where the loan money had gone. To widen a subsidiary market in *Europe.* Dan hadn't moved to take over, even though he'd been in the perfect position to do so.

Not a dime had gone to buy even one share of MacKenzie.

Phil stared at his phone. Rose would have to be told. She'd have to know in time to stop the counterattack on Garden King, in time to keep from ruining the man she loved.

Phil knew, was finally accepting, that he would always be Ashley Wilkes to her Scarlett, always needing her but never possessing the power to control the flames of Rose MacKenzie. He became more sure of those things as he gazed at his desk, seeing in his mind's eye the loneliness under the strength in Rose's eyes. He knew that, like so many women who took on the power of corporations in these times of equality, that Rose MacKenzie wanted something much simpler to complete her life.

When the phone rang, he jumped. He shook himself and grabbed for the receiver.

"Yes. Philip Van Dyke."

"Phil, this is McCall."

"Yes, Mac."

"I've got something new here for you. I think we've finally uncovered our missing link."

"Well, tell me, will you?"

"It's got to do with Red MacKenzie, and something that happened a long time ago. You know all this garbage about that will?"

"Yeah..."

"It's all real! Can you believe it? Nobody in the U.S. had any idea this garbage was happening. It involves a British account set aside for a woman—"

Phil sat forward. "For Rose?"

"No! I'll tell you who in a minute. You're not gonna believe what Rose's old granddaddy did to her and this Masters guy. You ready?"

"Mac, for Christ's sake, put me out of my misery, will you?"

"Okay, listen to this..."

Rose felt her resolve crumble.

Dan Masters was a wounded giant, standing there at the end of the shiny table, begging to know the reason for his execution.

Suddenly, no reason was enough. Nothing was worth this.

All she wanted to do was hold him. She wanted to press her body against his and assure him that all she wanted was his love and to give hers to him. Suddenly the business, the fortune, the future—it all meant nothing. Rose had crushed him and found she had crushed herself.

At that very moment, she snapped.

She knew she'd never take his company and she no longer cared if he tried to take hers. Nothing was worth seeing that look on Dan's face where only a few short days ago there had been nothing but desire.

Despite the angry, injured expressions of Dan's associates they were realizing there was something deeply personal going on here between the presidents of the two companies. This was the wild card. This wasn't a run-of-the-mill takeover. Because they didn't really know what to do about it right at the moment, they decided that maybe nothing for a time would be the wisest course.

They stared uncomfortably at the powerful woman and the powerful man she had just toppled. The pain in Dan's face went beyond the loss of a business, and that was scary to people who'd done business with him all these years. They'd never seen that expression before. A man standing tall on dignity alone.

None of this was lost on Rose. She saw and correctly interpreted it all. She parted her lips to speak, to tell him she didn't mean it anymore, that there had to be some misunderstanding at work here, that she knew him better than she had let herself think.

Before she could speak, Dan mutttered a feeble, "Excuse me—", gestured to his associates to wait, and turned quickly out of the conference room. He was too angry, or too injured, to throw out a dramatic exit line.

The space he left behind became a tomb.

"Dan—" Rose gasped. She shot a wave at her own people and snapped, "Stay here."

She dashed out into the office corridor and hurried down toward the elevators. When she came around the corner, there he was, walking away from her, very stiff and without any real direction. She'd just made sure he didn't even have an office to go back to—not officially, anyway.

"Dan, wait! Please..."

She started toward him, but as she reached the elevators, one of them popped open and Phil charged out. Rose hadn't even seen him since she'd gotten back from Scotland. It seemed, he too, had been avoiding her.

"Rose!" Phil gawked at her, then he looked down the corridor to where Dan had paused and half-turned. He deduced the situation and blurted, "Oh, no...I'm too late, aren't I? Dan! Please don't go!"

He held out his good arm.

Rose watched Dan, her mind suddenly divided.

Dan had been looking at Rose, giving new meaning to the phrase 'You're beautiful when you're angry.'

Now, he looked at Phil.

"I thought we were becoming friends," he said to him, his voice choked. "But this isn't the kind of thing friends do to each other."

An elephant sat down on Rose's chest. She actually gasped, it hurt so much.

Eyes like cobalt meteors turned from Phil to her once again, in a face fired by a wild promise of excitement that she now threatened to extinguish. She felt her shoulders and thighs knotting, wanting to hold him.

Dan was a magnificent picture of modern hero laced with touches of a bruised teenager.

"You're really ruthless," he murmured to her. He started to turn away again, to keep heading down the hall, but he hesitated, staring into the bare wall beside him. "My God, my company..."

Rose's heart cracked. Nearby, she heard the crack of Phil's.

Dan cleared his throat with distinct effort, and his hands found the pockets beneath his suit jacket. "I thought I might have to step aside someday...but not this soon," he murmured. "Just don't fire any of the people who've been working for me—that's all I ask."

He took a few steps down the corridor away from them, leaving them on the thin emotional ice they'd made for themselves.

A third time he turned. He looked only at Rose now. She had destroyed him absolutely, and at this very moment she was paying the price.

She wanted to comfort him, to make those lake-blue eyes rove her limbs without the sad desire that hung on her now.

Dan stared at her as though he'd never seen her before.

"The minute you saw something you didn't understand, you ripped my heart out like an animal."

Rose took a tentative step, but it was as though Dan was surrounded by a wall of thorns. "Dan... please... I don't want your company—"

Now he barreled forward, and shocked both her and Phil when he grabbed a painting of the very building they were standing in and tore it from the wall.

"Do you think that's the point? This? *This?* Is that what your limited little mind thinks I care about? Well, it's yours!" He stalked to her and shoved the painting into her hands so hard that he knocked her backward.

"Take it," he seethed. Cocooned in his own raw fury now, bottling it only because people who had depended upon him were within earshot, Dan stepped back away from Rose. "Just treat it better than you've treated me."

He continued to glare at her, as though seeing a new person, some creature, he'd never seen before.

"As much as I loved you before," he added, backing still farther away, "I despise you now."

For a final time he turned and started away.

Rose numbly watched him go. The cold metal frame in her hands, pressed against her body. She felt the astonished presence of Phil a few steps away, but this time there was no comfort at all from his being here.

Dan paused in his deliberate march out of her life. Turning his head every so slightly, he spoke.

"And you thought I was the one with a dark side."

"Good God," Phil breathed, "what've we done?"

It was a tone of horror, as though he felt everything Rose was feeling—that something untenable was going on here and she had become the criminal.

Dan had disappeared into another elevator down the hall. He hadn't even gone back to his office. It was still his, Rose knew, for she couldn't follow through on taking it from him. What used to be important to her wasn't important anymore.

Phil was staring guiltily at the closed elevator door that had swallowed Dan. "Oh, Rose...what've I done."

Rose slumped against the nearby wall, twice as destroyed as Dan had been.

"It wasn't worth it," she murmured. "I love him, Phil...I love him. What made me feel I had to ruin him?"

Phil turned to her, turned away, then turned back again. Lately everyone knew that damn dance.

Rose closed her eyes rather than see it again. Tears squeezed out and spurted onto her reddened cheeks.

"You didn't have to," Phil said.

Even with her eyes closed, Rose could hear the anguish in his voice.

Her eyes shot open. She stared at him. Years of practice in the business world, practice reading people's eyes and tones of voice came into play.

She pushed herself off the wall, still clutching the precious picture of Dan Masters' company headquarters.

"Phil..." she whispered. But no words were needed. She understood his expression. Guilt. Error. Regret.

Details weren't important. She saw the overview very clearly in his face. He did have the courage, at least, to face her, to let her read his eyes without looking away.

"Rose," Phil began, "I don't know how to tell you this..."

Without moving, almost without breathing, she responded, "I've been hearing that a lot lately, Phil. Don't say that to me anymore."

"Okay—you're right."

"What *is* all this?"

"It's your grandfather. It's all Red MacKenzie's doing," Phil said. "I couldn't believe it myself. I'm late because I was double-checking everything. But it's all true. Red MacKenzie divided his fortune back in the 1960s into an American account and a British account. The British account was under several different corporate titles—and Rose...it involved a separate will, and a separate *inheritance*."

Rose sank into one of the lobby chairs still gripping the picture.

"My...grandfather...had *two* wills?"

Phil tried to say yes, but only a nod came out.

"How is that possible?" Rose asked. "How is that legal?"

"It's not. Ordinarily, the latest will supercedes any made before it. But Red circumvented the law by having both wills drawn on the same day, three thousand miles apart. The counselors drawing the wills had no knowledge of each other, or of the other documentation—"

"Wait a minute!" She stumbled to her feet and paced the corridor. "Are you saying that it was my *Gran's idea* that Dan had to marry me?"

Phil paused, then stammered, "Yes...yes, that's about it."

"My Gran did that to me?"

"Apparently he did."

"What's Dan Masters got to do with my grandfather!"

Phil fell into sudden quiet, only mouthing *I don't know.*

"Whatever it was," he said, "you and I just killed it."

Chapter Sixteen

THE COUNTRYSIDE ONLY reminded her of Dan. Tall strong trees leaning with the wind, defying nature's pressing hand, yet all the while part of the scheme. Delicious, thrilling, painful.

Yes, there was pain. Phil's drive in the country wasn't helping to get rid of it. A knotting ache in the pit behind her breasts was just a hole where her heart was supposed to be. Her reflection in the right rearview mirror was that of a ghost, a beautiful but pale ghost, a mere spectre of womanhood.

She had left all her substance on a distant brae, in the hands of the man she'd betrayed.

She still loved him too much.

She quit looking at the sad goddess in the mirror. The landscape swirling by was much more appealing.

Beside her, Phil just drove the car. He hadn't said a word the whole time. Clearing their heads, he'd said. New York was far behind, and Rose didn't care what lay ahead anymore.

In fact, she'd neglected her work for the three days since the board meeting at Garden King. She'd sunken into that sad spectre and hadn't emerged, until finally Phil shook his head and dragged her into the car. That was enough, he'd said.

Rose knew this wouldn't change anything. It was hard going on with life in a loveless world, especially when love had been so close.

The contrast was blinding. As much as Rose had once prided herself on her survival instinct, now she was glad to let it go.

"I have to find him, Phil," she said suddenly.

Phil glanced at her. "Oh?"

"Whatever Gran caged him into has to end. Gran's dead now. I couldn't accept it...but now I can."

"Yes," Phil said. "And the wills he wrote went into effect the day he died. You sure you know what you want now?"

"I want to be free," she said. "And I want Dan to be free of the MacKenzie chains that have been on him."

She felt the highway wind race through her hair, flipping it across her cool cheeks in bright strands of red. She looked at Phil.

"Will you help me find him?"

The Connecticut countryside glowed with nature's patina; mossy shrubs and wildflowers spangled the sides of the smooth paved roadway lined with Colonial houses as old as the nation. It was an old road, narrow and unlined, without shoulders. The skirt of greenery came right up to the car. Butterflies did erratic dances in the turbulence left by the rushing car. New England surrounded them like a bouquet.

All at once Phil started slowing down, craning his neck at the side of the road.

After what seemed a long time, he said, "Yeah...I guess I might as well help you find him, Rose."

Quite suddenly, he was wheeling into a gravel driveway, near a split-rail fence.

"Turning around?" Rose asked.

"No," he said. "Not yet."

The Porsche rolled down the gravel drive and around a bend. The surroundings grew steadily less wild. Old trees and ferns gave way to an array of flowers and foliage that had been deliberately cultivated to merge with the frame of wild growth. Rose didn't recognize most of the blooms, but the garden was designed for color. An English garden, with flowers so thick no weeds could grow.

There was a pond, too, with swans.

For a moment, Rose forgot her misery. "Phil...look."

The swans curled their long necks at the sound of the car, but took no other notice as they skimmed between the lilies on the glassy pond.

"I think I was here in a fairy tale once," Phil commented as they came into view of a cottage. It was a thatched stone cottage just like in the stories, with a white picket fence, brick patheways, and even a rose-covered arbor.

Roses. Perfect azure blooms by the hundreds.

"Phil..."

Phil ignored her and pulled the car to a stop.

"Phil, where are we?" she persisted.

Turning to her with a touch of color on his cheeks, Phil said, "Get out of the car, Rose. Take a walk."

She studied him with her eyes narrowed, then she pushed the door open and got out onto the gravel driveway.

The thatched cottage sat warm and welcoming before her.

"Phil, what are you doing to me?"

"Well, he twisted my sore arm..." Phil said from inside the car. "Go on inside, Rose."

"Let's both go," she said.

He folded his arms and sank down in the seat. "Not me."

Sunlight glinted in Rose's hair—she could actually feel the warmth. Her emotions churned as she walked slowly toward the trellis and the cascade of blue blooms and buds.

She paused beneath another rose-covered arch.

Blue blooms made a halo all around her. On the trellis there was an engraved gold plaque, and all around it there were plastic signs...

THE ROSE MACKENZIE GRANDIFLORA BLUE

Champion Supreme, New England Horticulture Society
1988-89 1989-90 1990-91

All-American Rose Society Honors
1988, 89, 90

North American Hybridizers Rose-of-the-Year
1990, 91

Tiffany Collection Choice
1991

A large azure bloom curtseyed into her hand. She caressed it. Pure velvet.

The cottage door loomed before her. The gravel crunched under her shoes. She didn't look back.

The door was open for her.

Inside the cottage was charming. The walls were painted wood, the floor hardwood, dotted with braided rugs. The furniture had a country masculinity about it and a casual lack of theme. There was a TV set in an open Shaker cabinet, one obviously meant to be closed up sometimes. Shaker chairs and hutches and a fat sofa settled into a jumble of Amish, nautical, folk art and Colonial bits and pieces. Clearly a decorator had started things, but items and personal touches, however mismatched, had been added over time.

A tall shadowed form in the den made her heart quicken. Dan stood, his hands in his pockets, beside a cane-and-hickory rocking chair.

Rose stepped onto one of the braided rugs and folded her hands in front of her.

"I'm in love with your garden," she said softly.

He didn't turn.

"It was a product of inspiration."

The resonance of his voice chilled and warmed her at the same time.

Nodding thoughtfully, Rose simply murmured. "The cottage is nice, too."

He still didn't turn. "It's my house. I live here."

"I'm in love with your house."

He shifted his weight, and the sunlight from outside struck his shoulder differently. "It's comfortable for me."

Without moving farther into the den, Rose sent her feelings out toward Dan and knew, somehow, that he could read them.

"I'm in love with you."

She waited for a reaction. It was subtle. A change in the set of his shoulders, a slight bowing of his head as his eyes lost their focus on the pond view, a stiffening of his legs, his arms.

"I introduced myself to the roses on the trellis," she said.

"The Grandiflora Blues."

"The Rose MacKenzie Grandiflora Blues," she corrected. "The

name...is that for my benefit?"

"No," he admitted. "They've always been called that."

"How long is always?"

About four years since they've been pure blue."

She offered a faint smile and murmured, "You have quite a blue thumb."

"Thanks. It's getting bluer."

"Dan, I'm withdrawing my takeover bid. I don't want your business."

Dan spun around. "What?"

Rose felt tears push at her eyes. "You brought out my soul. It's yours now."

Strange how easily she had said it, how the words hadn't caught in her throat.

"I know now how important it is to trust," she said quietly. Then she started to leave.

"Rose," he called.

She stopped.

"What is this?" he asked. "A test?"

Rose turned and gazed back at him. Her voice softened almost to a whisper. "I've been betrayed by my grandfather. All I have left is Phil...and you."

Dan moved for the first time, crossing the stenciled floor. Until now, Rose wouldn't have been able to imagine Dan in a quaint English cottage surrounded by Hepplewhite tables and 19th-century candle molds. Now, though, he seemed suited to it and to the stone fireplace beside him. He leaned a palm on the mantel and leveled a gaze on her.

"That's what I was afraid you'd think about your grandfather," he murmured, shaking his head. "Phil told me you thought I was maneuvering to buy MacKenzie," he said evenly. "I never wanted your company. I wanted your *love*."

A big ice cube formed in her throat, and there was no way she could talk around it. "You wanted me to marry you to satisfy my own grandfather's second will. I know the whole story."

"No, you don't," he said.

Unable to speak, she simply planted her feet on the braided rug and waited.

Dan took a long preparatory breath, then dived headlong into the past.

"My family was living in Glasgow, where my mother was doing her graduate studies, when my father was suddenly transferred to Greenland. My mother stayed behind to let us kids finish out the school year and get ready to move."

"You were raised there?" Rose asked abruptly.

"No, I'm American. I told you that before. We were just there for a while. It also happened that your grandfather was in Glasgow at the same time. He and my dad were good friends. The two of them and John Henwoodie were in the service together during World War II. Red was like a second father to us."

Dan averted his eyes, unable to look at her any longer as he continued his story. There wasn't any shame in his voice, but not much pride either.

"Red's wife was in the U.S., with your father. Red was incredibly in love with her. My mother was also alone and lonely. In their need, they turned to each other. It was very sudden, very unexpected, and very short. Right afterward, we took off for Greenland and the whole thing was over. My parents maintained close contact with Red, and when my sister Anna was born, Red became her godfather. He and my mother silently bore the secret that he was also her father."

Rose gulped and blurted, "Your sister... is my grandfather's child?!"

Dan turned suddenly.

"Yes... but please don't make any judgments. Red was my guardian, my mentor. My second father, really. For some reason—probably because she knew how close I felt to Red—my mother told me about her relationship with him before she died, even though I was only eight years old. I never told my father. I never told Anna. I should've hated Red, but my reaction was to love him that much more. How could I fault him for needing love when he was lonely? I've needed the same thing."

The shock had come and gone some words ago. Rose accepted the whole idea faster and better than she could've predicted. Maybe she was changed, too.

"Honestly," he said, "I thought Red was kidding when he said he was going to make you marry me! He used to say that all the time—

and then he'd laugh. The British account was set aside for Anna... and for my company. Red was a silent partner. When he died and that will became active—God, I couldn't believe it. And I didn't know what to do to protect Garden King and the inheritance he'd left to my sister. She deserves the money. She's his child, And I didn't want to destroy your respect for Red, either." He paused, and looked at his toes like a little boy. "And...I was afraid that just looking at me might remind you of his infidelity."

He moved to a bouquet of the Blues on a small table and played the blooms like piano keys.

"Red always took care of me," he said. "He knew how I felt about you, but, believe me, Rose, I had no idea he was that crazy."

He moved back to the window.

"You had every right to jump to the conclusions you did, and it's my fault that you did. I guess I could wait until I'm forty and Red's marriage stipulation is no longer valid, but I don't think you'd wait for me that long. But maybe you'll believe me then, when I don't have anything else to lose. That's all I have to say...except that I still love you."

He turned and looked out over the pond again, and waited to be alone.

After all they'd been through, he didn't really expect to feel tapered fingers slide up his back. His spine tingled like bells caroling. His eyes drifted closed as though something was hurting him.

"Turn around," she murmured. The sound was dark velvet to him.

He shivered. "I can't. Rose, please go if you're going."

A second hand drifted up to his shoulderblade. "Do you really want me to leave?" she asked.

Raggedly he said, "You're killing me."

She whispered to him. "Let me kiss it better."

He turned, to see if this was really happening.

They amazed each other with a kiss like none they'd ever shared before. It was the most complete kiss two people could give each other. They were sure now, full of the trust they'd once spoken of without understanding it. Dan caught Rose in his arms and she received him in poignant rediscovery. They were crushing their bodies together, caressing each other, clutching so tight that she groaned against him and he sighed heavily in response. Sunlight reflected off the pond outside and shone upon the lovers. Dan held her back for a moment and looked at her. She encircled his face with her warm hands, gazing into the eyes that had loved her for so long.

"I love your garden, I love your house," she uttered softly, "and I love you."

His lips pulsated against hers. "Rose..."

She smiled, and pressed even closer against him. "What a pair we are. I was a one-person walled city, and you didn't exactly teach by example. We're both so rotten...we deserve each other."

"You mean..."

"I mean that if we aren't together," she said softly, "then somebody else might get stuck."

"Oh, God—" Dan closed his eyes quickly for a moment, afraid his intense adoration might burn her skin. He brushed aside a strand of her auburn hair. A huge sigh purged him of all disbelief. He pulled her away again, looked into her eyes to make sure it was true. It was. With a delirious shudder he drew her quickly into his arms, where she fit as though made for him.

Their clothing slid to the rug piece by piece, his sweater, her blouse, his jeans, her bra, until the clothes dangled about the room like Christmas decorations. Her pale shoulders were bared to his lips, to the gentle anxious moisture of his breath. She guided his hands to places on her body where she had never welcomed him before, not even in those lost moments of entangled passion in Scotland. She was giving herself utterly to him, and taking the wonders he offered.

After half a lifetime of hope, love finally came to the little thatched cottage with the trellised blue roses.

The sun had moved in the sky before either of them discovered time again.

They lay together before a stone fireplace much like the one in Castle Diath's cozy library, tangled in a rag quilt, and laughing like two children playing hookey. Somehow it all seemed so distant now—the distrust and all the little doubts that had held them apart.

Dan propped himself up on an elbow, gazed at Rose's lovely face nest in the fan of auburn curls, then leaned over and kissed her and kissed her again.

"Mmmmmm," he groaned. "You taste good."

"I feel good," she responded. She cupped her hand around the nape of his neck, beneath his golden hair, and said, "I feel right. I've never felt so right. If only Gran could see us now."

Dan laughed. "Right now?"

"That rotten old conniving warthog deserves what he gets. Besides, this is what he wanted!"

Dan's eyes grew misty then, as though he too was remembering her grandfather. He might actually have known a side of Red MacKenzie that Rose had never known. In that alone, Dan was suddenly special to her.

"Marry me, Rose," he murmured. "Marry the real me."

"Under the blue roses on the arbor," she said. "I'll wear my grandmother's wedding dress and I'll carry a bouquet of blue roses. You'll wear the MacKenzie kilt and dress doublet. Phil can give me away."

Dan smiled. "Phil shouldn't have to give you away. Sir John can do that. Phil should be best man...if he wants to be."

"Oh, Dan, you're the most—" All at once she sat up abruptly. "Phil!"

Dan draped another quilt over her shoulders and asked, "What?"

"He's still outside!"

A flush of color filled Dan's cheeks. "Oh..."

He pulled on his jeans and helped Rose up. As she wrapped herself quickly with the rag quilt, Dan went to the kitchen window and looked out.

"Is he there?" Rose called, still wrestling with the quilt.

"Beats me," Dan said, smiling. "All I see is a pair of Guccis sticking out of the car window."

Rose joined him, and together they gazed out through the blue roses on the arbor.

"Guess I'd better go get him," Dan said. "If he's as hungry as I am, he'll wither away to nothing out there before he'll come up and knock on the door."

"That's right," she said.

Dan turned to her, cradling her hips in his hands. "Say 'I will.'"

Rose brushed a russet lock out of her eye and gazed at him. "Hm?"

"Let me hear you say you'll marry me."

Strongly and fully, she said, "I will, Dan. I will marry you. I will, will, will."

Dan wrapped an arm around her and wove his fingers through her hair, for the closeness of her was all the gold he would ever need.

"After all this time," he murmured, "I finally found the perfect Rose."